# RED EYES IN THE DARKNESS

I peered into the darkness of the closet. It was completely black—except for two red lights winking on and off. They looked almost like eyes. I shuddered and blinked to clear my vision. Although I could no longer see them in the doorway, I could feel them watching me.

Jenn looked at me curiously. "What's the matter?" she asked.

I'm seeing things, I thought to myself, but aloud I replied, "Nothing. Why do you ask?"

She studied me a moment longer before replying, "I know this sounds weird, but you look like you've just seen a ghost."

**COME VISIT DRAGON SCHOOL AND MEET
THE KIDS OF THE DRAGON SCHOOL WEEKLY
ON THE INTERNET AT
WWW.DRAGONSCHOOL.COM**

# DRAGON SCHOOL

by
Cara J. Copperman

Illustrated by
John Pierard

Byron Preiss Multimedia Company, Inc.
New York

Pocket Books
New York  London  Toronto  Sydney  Tokyo  Singapore

## To My Parents

An *Original* Publication of POCKET BOOKS

POCKET BOOKS, a division of Simon & Schuster Inc.
1230 Avenue of the Americas, New York, NY 10020

Byron Preiss Multimedia Company, Inc.
24 West 25th Street
New York, New York 10010

The Byron Preiss Multimedia World Wide Web Site address is:
http://www.byronpreiss.com

The Dragon School Web Site address is http://www.dragonschool.com

ISBN 0-671-01180-4
First Pocket Books paperback printing October 1997
10 9 8 7 6 5 4 3 2 1
POCKET and colophon are registered trademarks of Simon & Schuster Inc.

Cover art by Steve Fastner
Cover design by Steven Jablonoski
Interior design by MM Design 2000, Inc.

Printed in the U.S.A.

# CHAPTER 1

"Hey, Jenn! I'm on my way out the door," I called through my bedroom window.

After a moment, Jenn's face appeared in the window of the house next door, her eyes barely open. "Where are you going?" she asked sleepily. Her blond hair was sticking out in all directions. She looked like she had been tumbling around inside a clothes drier.

"School, you nincompoop!" I yelled. "What happened to your hair?"

"School? Who goes to school on a Sunday? I'm going back to sleep." She ducked her head back through the window.

Not again! I thought to myself. Then I yelled, "It's Monday! Get up, you bum!"

Jenn's head popped back up in surprise. "Monday? Why didn't you say so?" she cried out frantically before disappearing with a crash. I heard a muffled "ouch," then Jenn reappeared, rubbing her head. "I'll be out in two minutes."

I shook my head, then turned back inside. Grabbing my baseball cap, I made my way to the kitchen. As usual, my mom was gone before I woke up. She left a note saying she would be studying late at the library again. Ever since she started teaching at the university full-time, her hours have gotten really long.

I stuffed a Pop-Tart in my backpack and left through the kitchen door, locking it behind me. Realizing I'd probably have a long wait, I walked over to Jenn's side door and sat on the stoop to eat my breakfast.

Now, Jenn is a lot of cool things. She's an excellent basketball player, plus she's my best friend. But one thing Jenn is not is on time. Our neighborhood is just a short distance from the Anthony T. Dragon Elementary School, so ever since pre-K, Jenn and I have walked the few blocks together. And ever since pre-K, Jenn has kept me waiting.

Luckily, it was nice out. Waiting for Jenn in cold weather was much less pleasant, even though winters in Northern California, where we live, never get too brutal. But fall was just barely on its way in, with a few October leaves on the ground to remind us that Halloween was right around the corner. Little did I suspect that I was in for a few premature scares within the next few hours.

"Are you sure it's Monday?" Jenn asked, bounding down the steps in her high tops and chewing a huge wad of gum.

"Maybe you need an alarm clock with a calendar," I suggested. I grabbed my backpack and stood up. "Fred has his computer programmed to wake him up on school days."

"Yeah, and how many times has he already been late this year?" Jenn looked back at me as she power-walked down the front lawn. She reached the sidewalk in just a few steps.

"Hey, Stretch, slow down. Some of us are vertically challenged," I called to her.

"Get over it, Benji. You're not short. You're average." She slowed as I caught up and then patted me condescendingly on the head.

She's right about the average thing. In fact, I'm the most average person in the fifth grade at Dragon School—average brown hair, average brown eyes, average looks. It's a good thing you don't need to be handsome to be a journalist, or I'd be out of luck. I am editor-in-chief of our school newspaper, the *Dragon School Weekly*, and someday I hope to be wiring in news reports from exotic places like Tripoli and Timbuktu.

I measured myself next to Jenn as we walked, figuring she was a good four inches taller than I was. "Did you grow overnight?" I asked with a straight face.

She smacked my head. "Shut up, you goon." Then her shoulders slumped. "I probably did, at that. My dad says if I outgrow another pair of jeans, he's going to make me start wearing skirts."

"Ohh. That's rough." I've known Jenn my whole life and I don't think I've ever seen her in anything but jeans or shorts.

At that moment, I felt a hand snatch my baseball cap from my head. I wheeled around to see Sly Wright, our very own, very large school bully, swinging the cap and laughing. "Nice hat, Phillips. Looks tiny enough for your pea-brained head."

I stormed over to him to grab the hat, but he held it over my head, just out of reach. "Come on, Sly, give it back," I said through clenched teeth. Every time I jumped up to reach it, he held it higher. What I really wanted to do was punch him in his stomach, but I restrained myself. I didn't want to have to explain another black eye to my mother. I'd already had two catastrophic run-ins with Sly that year.

"Come and get it, Benji Boy." He dangled the hat over my head, his fat, freckled face leering at me.

Jenn went over to him and tried to snatch it from his hands. "Cut it out, you stupid creep!"

He kept it away from her by holding it higher above his head. "Oh, Benjamina can't stick up for herself and has to get Dr. J. to fight for her."

Jenn turned to Sly and yelled, "Why don't you go pick on someone your own size, you big baboon!"

Sly tossed the cap to me over Jenn's head, laughing. "It's your lucky day, Phillips. I'm giving you a break. I just came from the schoolyard. And believe me, you've got bigger things to worry about this morning." He waggled his eyebrows mysteriously and stalked off to torment another kid across the street.

Jenn chomped furiously on her gum. "Of all the kids in school to get left back in fifth grade, why did it have to be Sly Wright?"

"Bad karma?" I said. I put my cap on my head and jogged next to her, trying to keep up with her fast-paced walk. "What do you think he meant by saying we have bigger things to worry about?" I asked nervously.

"I'm sure it's nothing," Jenn said, snapping her gum thoughtfully. "You know Sly. He's the classic middle child—he does things just for the attention."

"But Sly's an only child," I pointed out.

"Oh," she said thoughtfully. "Well, then maybe he's just a jerk who likes to hear himself talk."

"I'd buy that for a nickel. But I'm still nervous. Sly has had it in for me ever since that bake sale last year when I saw him steal the money."

"But you weren't the one who snitched on him."

"I know that and you know that. Sly probably knows it too, but he'd rather torture me. He needs someone to blame for all the trouble he got in."

Out of the corner of my eye, I saw a colorful streak come whizzing down the street.

"Heads up!" Bonnie called out in a squeaky voice.

"Whoa!" I stuck out my arm in time to catch her before she rolled right past us. "Still learning to use the brakes on those in-line skates, huh, Bonnie?"

"I'm working on it," she said breathlessly, tucking stray red curls back into her helmet. "I've gotten pretty good. Watch." She skated into the street and spun around twice, her bright green skirt flaring out, then headed back our way. Jenn caught her before she sped into a prickle bush.

"How did you get so good without ever learning to stop?" Jenn asked Bonnie as she skated on the sidewalk beside us.

"Why stop when you can twirl instead? I can always find something to grab onto—people, trees, furniture, whatever." She giggled and jumped the curb in front of us, spinning around in the middle of the street. Luckily, there was hardly any traffic in our neighborhood at eight o'clock in the morning.

"Hey, how did your gymnastics meet go last night?" Jenn asked Bonnie as we caught up with her on the other side of the street.

"Not so good." She wrinkled her nose as she grabbed hold of my backpack so I could pull her along as I walked. "We came in fourth," she added.

"Fourth place isn't so bad," Jenn consoled her. "How many teams were in the meet?"

"Four." Bonnie laughed, then saw Jenn's grimace and said, "It's okay, really. It was fun. Even when I blew my dismount off the uneven parallels, I only landed on my gym bag. Nobody else was in the way."

Jenn winced, then turned to us suddenly. "Hey, I just remembered. Did you guys hear about what happened at the PTA meeting on Friday?"

"No, what?" Bonnie asked innocently.

Not again, I thought. "Bonnie, weren't you supposed to be covering the meeting for the paper?" I asked.

"Oops. Sorry, Mr. Editor." Bonnie blushed and twirled one of her long red curls around her finger. "I sort of forgot."

"That's okay," Jenn said, rushing in before I could get angry. "I went with my dad. Part of our father-daughter bonding evening." She made a face. "I can write up something. . . ."

Good old Jenn, coming through in the clutch, I thought. "So what happened?" I asked.

"Well," she said, dramatically blowing a big bubble and letting it pop loudly before she continued. "It was a pretty big deal. First one of the parents announced that about five cases of food were discovered missing from the school cafeteria last week."

"That's not a big surprise," I said sarcastically. "The food probably got up and walked away by itself to spare us the torture of having to eat it."

"Do you really think so?" Bonnie asked with a straight face.

Jenn shot me a look that said, "Go suck on a rag." "Bonnie, get a clue. He was just trying to be funny."

Bonnie giggled. "Of course he was." She looked at me as if she wasn't certain, then turned back to Jenn. "So, well, what did happen to the food?"

"No one knows," Jenn continued. "But about the same time the granola bars started to disappear—one case each day—the librarian began finding a big mess when she opened up the library in the morning—books toppled on the floor and even some bookshelves overturned."

"How come we didn't hear anything about it?" I asked.

"Well, that's where the weird part comes in," Jenn said. "The school board kept it hush-hush because they didn't want to cause a panic. The buzz among the parents after the announcement was that the ghost of Anthony T. Dragon has come back to haunt the school."

"A ghost?" Bonnie turned to stare wide-eyed at Jenn and bumped into a tree in the middle of the sidewalk.

"That's what some people are saying," Jenn replied uncertainly. She helped Bonnie up from the ground and explained, "There haven't been any incidents in twenty years, but some of the parents who were students at Dragon School in the seventies remember things just like this happening back then, too."

"You sound as if you actually believe the rumors," I said in disbelief.

"Maybe I do." Jenn frowned at me. "You know, for a person who claims to be the world's next big reporter, you certainly don't have an open mind, Benji."

"There are certain things you don't need to have an open mind about," I said, angrily kicking a small pile of leaves. "Ghosts don't exist. ESP doesn't exist. Monsters don't exist. End of story. As long as you're thinking the Boogie Man is after you, you're never going to get to the bottom of any story, no matter how good a reporter you are, Jenn."

I looked up and realized we had stopped in front of Fred Teller's house. He's the other member of our four-person newspaper staff and can usually be counted on to take my side in arguments.

"How much do you want to bet Fred isn't up yet?" Jenn asked, giving me a knowing look.

Just then, Fred appeared from the side of his house, carrying his skateboard. "I'll remember that, Jenn. Some friend you are." He laughed and jumped onto his board, skating down the steps of his house. "I'm a new person these days, on time and everything."

"No, you're still the same old Fred," Jenn said, looking at his mop of unbrushed curly brown hair. "Your shirt's untucked and you've got jelly on your face."

He shrugged one shoulder and didn't bother trying to fix anything.

"Get in trouble for being late again last week?" I asked.

"How did you guess?" he said, skating beside us on the street. Fred moves more naturally on wheels than most people do on foot. He got a skateboard and a computer for his birthday in second grade, and ever since he's been a whiz at both. "One more 'tardy' and I'll have to stay after school and clean erasers for Nerdy Thurdy." He ollied up a curb, sailed into the air, and landed gracefully on the sidewalk in front of us.

"There's nothing worse than spending quality time with our beloved vice principal," I said, sympathizing.

"Yes, actually there is," Fred replied. "I'd have to stay after with Sly."

"Now that's brutal," Jenn said.

"Too bad you missed him. We just had the pleasure of his company," I added.

"Already?" Fred asked. "Looks like he's getting up earlier these days, too."

"What happened?" Bonnie asked.

I let out a frustrated breath and explained, "Let's just say, it's not even eight-thirty on a Monday morning, and I can't see how this day, not to mention this week, can get any worse." I didn't want to have to relive the Sly incident all over again.

We had reached the side of the school and were about to turn onto the sidewalk that led into the front entrance. Fred rounded the corner ahead of us. Just as quickly, he picked up his skateboard, ducked, and walked back. "Uh-oh."

"Teller, come back here," a familiar but unwelcome voice rasped from the direction of the school. "And bring your other pals from the newspaper, too, since they're probably with you—especially Benjamin Phillips."

"I think you spoke too soon, Benji," Bonnie said.

I turned the corner, trying hard to keep a fake smile on my face as I looked at the vice principal. Looking back over my shoulder, I whispered to the others, "Yup. I think the day just got worse."

# CHAPTER 2

"What do you think he wants?" Bonnie whispered, stopping to change from her skates to sneakers.

"I have no idea," I mouthed silently. Vice Principal Thurdy was a really strange guy. On his first day of school, I had gone to his office to interview him for a "welcome" piece for the *Dragon School Weekly*. As soon as I asked him my first question—what he thought about two-hour lunch breaks—he flew into a rage and slammed the door in my face. Ever since then, he's given me a scowl whenever he's seen me. I figured he doesn't believe in the freedom of the press.

As we approached the entrance to the school, it occurred to me how appropriate Thurdy's nickname was: the Night Creature. With thin slitted eyes, pale greenish skin, and a permanent frown, Tyron Thurdy looked like he never slept and wasn't very happy about it.

"What's going on, Mr. Thurdy?" Bonnie asked casually.

"Principal Mullins would like to see all of you in his office," Mr. Thurdy said, sounding almost happy. "Immediately." He made an abrupt about-face and marched back toward the front door.

Jenn chomped anxiously on her gum as Fred bit his thumbnail. Bonnie stood in one place, swinging her skates back and forth. The three of them were obviously waiting for me to make the first move. I shrugged my shoulders and wordlessly followed Thurdy. They fell into place behind me.

"What does Mr. Mullins want to see us about, Mr. Thurdy?" Jenn called out. She hid her chewing gum, tucking it into her cheek with her tongue.

"You'll know when you get there," Thurdy said over his shoulder. Then he muttered under his breath, "As if you don't know already."

We exchanged worried glances and followed him into the school, a confused yet quiet procession. Finally we got to the door of the principal's office. As Thurdy turned the handle to walk in, I whispered to Jenn, "You'd think he would have read us our rights by now."

Taking a big, brave breath, I walked in as confidently as I could. But what I saw made me stop in my tracks. I could feel behind me that the others did the same.

"Glad you all could make it," the principal said from behind his desk. A tall man with a head like a pumpkin, bald and round, Mr. Mullins always had a smile on his face. Well, almost always. This time, his mouth was set in a grim line, an expression usually reserved for his conversations with Sly. "Allow me to introduce you to Officer Hunter," the principal said in a baritone I'd never heard him use before. He motioned to the uniformed woman standing by the window. Her dark-blue uniform could only mean one thing: She was a police officer.

She was tall with an athletic build and a hard, angular face. The officer nodded briefly and took out a notepad, moving as efficiently as a soldier.

"This is the staff of the school newspaper," Principal Mullins told her. Then he turned his attention back to us. "It seems there was a break-in last night."

"Someone got into the school?" Jenn asked in a shocked tone. "What happened?"

"Someone tampered with the entire computer system, either from inside or by remote," Officer Hunter replied abruptly. "We're looking into it."

Fred looked horrified. Ever since they installed the school computer system a year before, Fred had felt personally responsible for it. No one else, not even the teachers, knew as much about computers as he did. He was the one Mr. Mullins usually called when one of the computers went down.

"What did they do to my system?" Fred croaked.

"Your system?" the officer asked, surprised.

"That's what we wanted to ask you about, Fred." Mr. Thurdy said at the same time. "What did happen to *your* computer system?" He glared at each of us as if he thought we were hiding something. Officer Hunter looked suspiciously at Fred, and began taking notes.

"I have no idea what you're talking about," Fred said. His face drained of color.

"*Someone* crashed the entire system." The vice principal made it sound as though he knew exactly who that someone had been. "When we turned it back on, we found that the records for the entire fifth grade had been completely wiped out." An evil smile flashed across Thurdy's face, then disappeared just as quickly.

"Whoa!" said Bonnie. "That's serious." The rest of us gasped in surprise. I wondered briefly whether that meant the C I got in penmanship last year would disappear for good.

"Only someone with the right access code could have gotten to the student records," Fred said thoughtfully.

"Or someone extremely familiar with the computer system," Thurdy retorted.

I looked at Thurdy and a terrible thought came to mind: I'll bet he thinks we did it. I had to pull myself together and think like a reporter. "Do you think it has something to do with the other nighttime break-ins?" I asked, trying to remain cool.

The officer looked up from her pad as though she

was annoyed that she wasn't the one asking the questions. "And who might you be?" she asked me sharply.

"I might be . . . I mean I am Benjamin Phillips. I'm the editor of the student paper," I stammered.

"So you are the one with the keys to the computer room?" she asked pointedly.

I nodded, unsure whether speaking would get me out of trouble or deeper into it.

Principal Mullins took a deep breath. "Yes and no," he said hesitantly. "The four of them, as the staff of the school paper, share one set of keys for the computer room, but they're equally responsible for them."

Officer Hunter raised her eyebrows. "You're all equally responsible?"

Jenn spoke up quickly. "What the principal means is that whoever needs the keys at the time is in charge of them." Fred went back to chewing nervously on his thumbnail.

The officer turned to Jenn. "And what need do you have for these keys?"

"Well, um, actually Fred is the main troubleshooter for the school computers," Jenn began. "So he needs them a lot."

"I see." The policewoman looked over at Fred, who straightened up under her glare. She then scribbled something on her pad.

"But we all need to get into the basement, to get to the computer room, so we can lay out the newspaper," Jenn continued. Her words came out in a flood as the officer took more notes. "And sometimes we need to use the photocopier or the fax machine when we're researching stories," she concluded, out of breath.

Officer Hunter put down her pen and addressed the principal. "These kids certainly have a lot of responsibility for fifth-graders."

Principal Mullins looked at us as if he were greatly disappointed. It was the way he'd looked when Jenn and I were in first grade and had forgotten to feed the gerbil we'd taken home over the weekend. The gerbil had survived, but we'd had to clean erasers for a week.

He cleared his throat. "I have always had a great deal of trust in these four students," the principal said. "I have known them since they joined us in pre-K." He glanced nervously at the vice principal and then at Officer Hunter. "I've never had any reason to mistrust them in the past," he added almost apologetically.

Mr. Thurdy looked at us in disgust and then turned to Officer Hunter. "I have been telling Principal Mullins that he gives the children way too much authority. They have access to things that are too important to be trusted to *students*." He spat out the last word as though it left a bad taste in his mouth.

The officer's gaze took in each of us as she asked, "Who has the keys now?"

Mr. Thurdy stood with his arms folded across his chest, looking at Fred as though the answer were already perfectly clear. We all stood there in silence, waiting for the others to say something first. Fred stared down at his boots. The bell rang, but no one made a motion to go anywhere. Bonnie opened her mouth to say something but then closed it again.

"Bonnie?" the principal said encouragingly.

"I gave them to Fred on Friday," Bonnie said reluctantly. When no one responded, she continued, "Fred, you said you needed them to edit a story over the weekend, remember?"

"Yeah. I got the keys from you on Friday, but . . ." He looked as though he were searching for an excuse. "I didn't get to come in to the computer room because I went to my grandma's in San Francisco for the weekend instead." The words came out in a rush, and Fred breathed a sigh of relief.

We stood there without speaking, the silence broken only by the scratch of Officer Hunter's pencil on her notepad. She finally finished writing and looked up. "Mr. Thurdy, I'd like to see the computer room once again." It seemed more of a demand than a request. The officer turned toward the door, expecting the vice principal to follow behind.

"Anything I can do to help . . ." Thurdy looked

at us with an unspoken threat in his narrowed eyes. "Anything at all." He scurried out the door, trailing eagerly behind her.

The door clicked shut and the four of us stood uncomfortably in front of the principal's desk.

"Does anyone have any leads to who did it?" I ventured.

Jenn shot me a look. Perhaps I should have kept my mouth shut.

"Unfortunately, Benjamin, we do." Although he addressed his comment to me, the principal looked directly at Fred. "But we still don't have any hard proof." He got up from his desk and walked over and put his hand on my shoulder. I had the sinking feeling that I knew what was coming.

"I trust you kids," Principal Mullins said, "and I have to be honest with you, you're in big trouble. You four are the only students with unlimited access to the network, and the only ones with keys to the school. The best thing I can recommend is that you try your hardest to find out what really happened. If anyone can figure it out, you kids can."

Principal Mullins opened the door to show us out. "I'll do what I can to help, but I can't promise much," he added softly.

# CHAPTER 3

After the principal's door had clicked shut behind us, I turned to Fred angrily. "You didn't go to San Francisco this weekend, you were playing basketball with me on Saturday! What's wrong with you?"

Fred looked pained. "I was going to go in late Sunday afternoon to work on the computer, but I lost the keys," he said quietly.

"You lost the keys?" I shouted. Two kids passing by looked at us curiously. I lowered my voice. "How did you manage that?"

"I don't know." He looked down at his boots. "On Friday afternoon, I went to the Pizza Zone, you know, where I work sometimes. I was helping Angelino set up the new pinball game." He chewed his lip nervously. "I lost them either when I was under the machine to change the settings or when I wiped out on my skateboard on the way home."

Just then, Sly appeared from behind a pillar in the center of the hallway. "So, the great skateboard ace finally wiped out, huh?" By the crafty smile on his face, I was sure he was up to something. I hoped he hadn't heard any other part of our conversation. If he found out about the missing keys, we'd be in even bigger trouble. As if reading my mind, Sly added, "Carelessness killed the cat, my friends. I'd watch out, if I were you."

I opened my mouth to answer when a door nearby creaked open and Ms. Wilson, the school psychologist, called to Sly. "If you're through with your tantrum, Orville, we can continue our discussion now."

"Orville," Jenn repeated, snickering. "Why doesn't he make like Orville Wright and fly away?" she muttered.

Sly shot her a dirty look. He turned to us, speaking quietly enough for our ears alone. "It looks like the noose is finally on the other foot, huh, boys and girls? And I have a hunch things are going to get much worse for all of you very soon." He gave us an evil grin, then turned to Ms. Wilson, speaking sweetly. "Coming, Ms. Wilson."

As the door closed behind them, we all let out a big sigh. "He's really scary," Jenn said as we began walking down the corridor to our classrooms.

"You mean scary like he frightens you, or scary like he's totally out there?" I asked.

Jenn pondered this for a moment, then said, "I guess both, come to think about it."

"Do you think Sly heard about the keys?" Bonnie said, sounding worried.

"I'm sure he didn't." I tried to reassure her and

myself at the same time, but it didn't really work.
I was about to go off on Sly but remembered we had
more important things to discuss. Turning abruptly
to Fred, I whispered harshly, "Why didn't you just
tell Mullins you lost the keys?"

"If I told him, we'd lose key privileges and maybe
even get kicked off the paper." He looked over at
me and added, "I know sometimes I make mis-
takes, but even I could figure that one out."

I felt dumb for jumping on him like that. "Sorry.
I guess I'm not thinking straight," I said.

"Well, have you gone back to the pizza place to
see if Angelino found the keys?" Jenn asked, chang-
ing the subject.

"Not yet. I thought I'd go today after school,"
Fred replied. We all stood there glaring at him.
"Hey, how was I supposed to know someone would
hack into the system over the weekend?" he asked
defensively.

"So what do we do now?" Bonnie asked.

"Maybe we should check out the main computer room for clues," I suggested.

"Nice thought, Einstein. But without the keys,
we have no way of getting into the room," Jenn said
sarcastically.

I held my tongue, but a slow smile spread across
my face as I remembered something.

"What are you grinning about?" Bonnie asked. "If

you haven't noticed, this isn't a very funny situation."

"I've got the original set of keys." I mentally gave myself two points for that brilliant idea.

"You do?" they all asked at once.

"I figured that with four people sharing one set of keys, someone was bound to either lose them or get themselves locked in or out of somewhere. I kept the original set, and you guys have been using the copy."

"So I lost the copy? That means Thurdy and the police don't have to know we lost a set." Fred's face brightened for a moment, then he frowned again. "But it still looks to them like we trashed the system."

Jenn patted him on the back. "Don't worry about it. We just have to find the keys and then we can solve this mess."

"So, what should our plan of action be?" Bonnie asked.

I answered in my editor's voice, the one I used when handing out assignments for the paper. "Let's meet at the playground during lunch. In the meantime, talk to the other kids and find out what they know about what's been going on. And talk to people about those ghost rumors."

Fred relaxed a bit, as did the other two. I guess it helped them to think we were all working on this together, but I still felt the pressure that they were all counting on me more than each other.

"We'd better get to class," I said, starting to walk down the hallway. Jenn and I were in Mr. Reinhart's class together, and Bonnie and Fred were in the other two fifth-grade classes. "See you guys later."

The doors closed behind Bonnie and Fred as they each went into their rooms. Just then, I caught something out of the corner of my eye. I stopped and looked around, only to see an empty hallway and the janitor's closet door standing ajar.

I peered into the darkness of the closet. It was completely black—except for two red lights winking on and off. They looked almost like eyes. I shuddered and blinked to clear my vision. Although I could no longer see them in the doorway, I could feel them watching me. I was definitely letting the stress get to me.

Jenn looked at me curiously, her head tilted to one side. "What's the matter?" she asked.

I'm seeing things, I thought to myself, but aloud I replied, "Nothing. Why do you ask?"

She studied me a moment longer before replying, "I know this sounds weird, but you look like you've just seen a ghost."

\*   \*   \*

"Benji, can you answer the question?" Mr. Reinhart's deep, booming voice broke through my concentration.

I looked up, startled from my thoughts. "Five cases of granola bars," I replied without thinking. The class laughed and I realized I had been caught not paying attention again. It was a few hours after our trip to the principal's office that morning, and I was still spaced-out.

"Actually the answer is that a seesaw is an example of a class-one lever, but thanks for the creative answer," the teacher said, his round belly shaking as he laughed.

The bell rang for lunch, and everyone made a mad dash for the door. I was getting up to leave as quickly as possible when I heard my name called.

"Benjamin, can you please stay behind for a moment?" Mr. R. asked. "I'd like to speak with you."

Jenn, standing next to me, gave me a sympathetic smile. "I'll tell the others you're on your way," she whispered. "Good luck."

I nodded, took a deep breath, and walked to Mr. R's desk. Perhaps if I just acted apologetic, I hoped, I could get out of the conversation quickly.

Mr. Reinhart folded his hands in front of him and looked at me with concern, his mouth a thin line within his dark, bearded face. "Benjamin, is everything okay?"

I shrugged my shoulders. "Everything's fine, Mr. R. I just didn't get enough sleep last night. Sorry about messing up in class."

I tried to make it sound convincing, but he still looked worried. "I'd like to believe you," he said meaningfully and motioned for me to have a seat. "But Mr. Thurdy told me all about the hack-in."

I should have expected that, I thought to myself, but I let him continue.

"I don't know the other two kids on the paper, but I told him I couldn't see you or Jenn doing something so destructive. Or so illegal," he added with a frown.

"Thanks," I muttered. Thurdy really had it in for us, trying to turn our own teachers against us.

"I can't get involved in your problem, Benji," Mr. Reinhart went on, but I do want to warn you: You have to do what you need to in order to clear your names. Mr. Thurdy is convincing other teachers in the school that you're guilty, too."

Mr. R. walked over to the window and stared out at the yard. It seemed as though he didn't want to face me. I gathered my books wordlessly and headed off for the door. As I was about to walk out, he spoke, his back still turned. "Just don't let your schoolwork suffer."

Without answering, I closed the door softly behind me.

# CHAPTER 4

It was late into lunchtime by the time I got outside. There were just a few stragglers left at the picnic benches, finishing up their lunches, while the other kids were running around wildly. I headed for the old-fashioned metal jungle gym at the far edge of the field. It was where the newspaper staff always met. The other kids almost always left us alone on it.

As I made my way over to the meeting place, I could see Jenn, Bonnie, and Fred, all in their usual spots. Jenn, afraid of heights, was seated cross-legged on the ground beside the jungle gym; Fred was perched on the side of the structure, on the lookout for any trouble; Bonnie had already finished her macrobiotic-super-vegetarian lunch and was hanging upside down like a bat, arms folded across her chest, "digesting," she always said.

As I climbed up to my spot in the middle of them all, I told them about my meeting with Mr. Reinhart, and how he said that Thurdy was convincing people that we were responsible for crashing the computer system.

"That's pretty grim," Fred said after I'd finished talking.

"I just can't figure out why Thurdy seems to have it in for us," I said, thoughtfully munching a handful of potato chips.

"Yeah, first someone hacks into the school computers, then Thurdy convinces half the school that we did it, and now there's these ghost sightings," Jenn said. All eyes turned to her expectantly.

"What ghost sightings?" I asked, taking a bite of my tuna sandwich. I still wasn't sure about those red lights I'd seen in the janitor's closet, so I tried to appear casual, like I was more interested in my sandwich than in the ghost.

"Haven't you guys been keeping your eyes and ears open?" Jenn looked at our blank faces disapprovingly. "Boy, for a bunch of people who are supposed to be reporters . . ."

"What is it, already?" Fred asked impatiently.

"Well, I talked to a bunch of kids before lunch, and they're convinced the ghost of Anthony Dragon has come back to haunt the school," Jenn said, her eyebrows raised dramatically.

"That's nothing new," I said with a snort.

"Maybe not, but lots of kids are claiming they've actually seen him. Penny Asher was so freaked out the nurse sent her home."

I almost lost my grip on the bars. "What have they seen?" I tried hard to keep my voice from cracking.

31

Jenn looked at me searchingly. "All the reports differ," she said, taking a bite of her brownie. "The one thing that was consistent, though, was the red eyes."

I choked on my sandwich. Fred jumped up and pounded me on the back while I coughed and sputtered. Jenn looked at me sternly. "Okay, Phillips. Out with it."

"What?" I croaked.

"You saw something, didn't you?" She glared at me, hands on hips.

"Maybe," I said sullenly, "but it could have been anything."

"Maybe it was the ghost," Bonnie said, wide-eyed.

"Bonnie, you're a reporter. You're not supposed to believe rumors until you get the facts." I sighed.

"What did you see, Benjamin?" Jenn asked in a no-nonsense tone.

"It was nothing," I said into my sandwich. "Just a couple of red blinking dots in a dark closet."

"Whoa! Man! Did you feel anything weird?" Fred asked excitedly. "I bet you felt tingles and stuff, right?"

"You believe there's a ghost, too?" I asked in surprise.

Fred scratched his head. "Well, it's something we can't rule out."

"I'm with Fred on this one," Bonnie said.

"What about you, Jenn?" I asked.

"The thing is," she said, chewing her gum thoughtfully, "I don't know why the ghost would start bothering us now."

"And that's your only reason?" I cried in disbelief. "There's no such thing as ghosts," I said impatiently. "And even if there was a ghost crashing the computers, erasing grades, and knocking down books in the library, what about the missing granola bars? Ghosts don't need to eat if they're dead!"

"Maybe he was stealing from us to give to some kids who don't have any food," Bonnie chimed in.

"You're forgetting the point. Ghosts don't exist." My patience was wearing thin. I wanted to get started solving this case already.

Bonnie cut in. "Well, I believe in ghosts. I don't care what you say." She ignored my glare and went on. "There are a lot of things that can't be explained by science, but that doesn't mean that the supernatural doesn't exist. Maybe what everybody saw wasn't a ghost, but there could be some other force or being out there that doesn't follow the same rules of nature that we do."

"She is right, you know," said an unfamiliar voice. We all looked over in surprise at the boy who had suddenly appeared beside the jungle gym. "I am sorry for interrupting you," he said, "but I could not help overhearing your discussion. I am Alex

Chan. I recently moved here from China." He spoke with just a hint of an accent.

"Hey, Alex." Jenn, who has always been the friendliest one of our group, was the first to recover from the surprise. "I'm Jennifer Jeffries, but everyone calls me Jenn. We're, um . . ." She paused to think. "We're having a staff meeting of the school paper."

Good recovery, Jenn, I thought.

"This is Benjamin Phillips," Jenn continued. "He's our fearless leader." I nodded a polite hello, wishing we could get back to business. "Over there is Bonnie McCloud, our resident political activist and gymnast," Jenn added.

"Yes, Bonnie and I have met," Alex said.

"Hi, Alex." She pulled herself upright and waved to him from her place on top of the jungle gym. "We're in the same class," she explained to us.

Jenn went on. "The big guy over there is Fred Teller, computer genius."

"Yeah, and doofus in everything else," Fred muttered under his breath.

Bonnie kicked him, as she always did when he put himself down.

"It is nice to meet all of you," Alex said, pushing his glasses up on his nose. "I have been here at school for two weeks, but this is my first time out at recess. Previously, I have been in ESL class at this time."

"What's ESL?" Bonnie asked, swinging herself upside down again.

"English as a Second Language." Alex rolled his eyes. "After I spent ten days correcting the papers of every other student in the class, the teachers finally admitted that my English is superior to theirs. They have now allowed me to join the rest of the students."

"You barely have an accent. Where did you learn to speak so well?" Jenn asked.

"Before my family lived in China, I lived for a while in India. Before that, England." He saw our amazed looks and explained. "We move around a lot. My father is a diplomat. He represents the Chinese government and gets stationed all over the world. "

Jenn leaned forward, her eyes wide with admiration. "Wow. You've traveled all over the world?"

He waved his hand as if it were nothing. "Oh, yes. You know, all places begin to look the same after you have traveled as widely as I have," he said with a bored sigh.

Bonnie looked at him sympathetically. "You poor thing. It must be so difficult for you, moving around so much."

Alex shrugged his shoulders. "I have never had much trouble finding friends. My fear is that living in a small town such as Somerset might be too quiet after living in some of the biggest cities in the world."

"Hey, Somerset is very interesting," I spoke up, defending my hometown. "We're a half-hour from San Francisco, and there's a ton of history around here. This used to be a mining town."

"I apologize, Benjamin. I did not mean to offend you," Alex said coolly. "I know all about San Francisco—it's where my father works. I am actually quite a history buff. One way I amuse myself when I move to a new location is to study the town I live in. So far, Somerset seems fascinating." He didn't look too convinced—at least, to me he didn't.

Jenn smiled warmly and said, "I'd be happy to show you around."

"What were you saying about the supernatural, Alex?" I asked, trying to bring us back to our main issue.

"Well, I come from a very traditional Chinese family. We believe very strongly in the spirit world, and I must say you are ignoring a lot of what goes on in the universe if you believe in only what you can observe."

Oh, brother, I thought, isn't anyone on my side in this one?

Alex continued. "My father says that many people today, all over the world, do not believe strongly in anything, and that is why they can never see things that are right in front of their faces."

"So you're saying that you have to believe in

something in order to see it, and not the other way around?" Bonnie asked.

Alex nodded and said, "Some things. Things that require more than just your eyes to notice them."

"Like spirits," Bonnie said triumphantly. " I told you guys."

"Sit up, Bonnie, you're turning purple," Fred said.

Bonnie sat up. "I need to hang upside-down. It helps me think better."

Maybe I should try it, I thought to myself. I didn't seem to be having much luck in the brains department today. I looked at the clock above the door and realized lunch was almost over. I needed to regroup and get everyone focused on what we had to do. "Look, guys, this is all very interesting, but we've got a mystery to solve."

"I would like to help you," Alex offered. "Is there something I can do?"

"It would be great if you could help us, Alex," Jenn said eagerly. I shot Jenn a look, but she continued, ignoring me. "We've got a little problem. . . ."

"Yes, I know about your difficulties with Mr. Thurdy. I was listening to your conversation. I hope you don't mind." He didn't seem at all apologetic for eavesdropping.

Bonnie twirled over the bar she had been sitting on and jumped to the ground. "Would you really help us, Alex? We need all the support we can get."

Fred looked at me and shrugged. "It might be good to have a new point of view."

"It's a free country," I said, giving up. "If you really want to hang with us, Alex, that's great. But you're probably going to end up in the thick of it with the rest of us if we can't prove our innocence."

There was a brief silence as Alex seemed to consider my words. "I will take that risk. I do not like to see people treated unfairly," Alex announced gallantly. "Besides, it would also be a good way to learn more about your interesting town."

The warning bell rang, signaling it was almost time to go in, and we climbed down the jungle gym. "Well, as long as that's settled, let's all get together tonight in the conference room at seven o'clock for a special meeting," I said quickly, then explained to Alex, "We meet on the Internet in a virtual conference room a couple of evenings a week to work on the paper. Tonight we should get together so we can figure out a game plan."

"Can you get on-line from home, Alex?" Jenn asked, cracking her gum.

"Not yet. We had a lot of things shipped here from China that have not yet arrived. Unfortunately, our computer was among them."

"Oh," Jenn said. She furrowed her brow in thought, then brightened up. "Why don't you go to Benji's house?" She turned to me. "Benji, you've got two computers. You and Alex can chat with us from your house. It's the easiest setup." She didn't wait for my consent. "Benji can write down his address for you, Alex."

Jenn could be pretty persuasive at times. Or was the word "pushy"? Four is fine. Five is a crowd, I was telling myself, but I kept silent.

Alex flashed a confident grin. "That would be terrific, Jenn, as long as Benjamin doesn't mind."

Neither of them looked to me for an answer; they both simply started for the school building. I held back my objections. No one seemed to have noticed this guy's arrogance but me. I wrote down my address and phone number and handed it to Alex. "No problem, man," I said, smiling weakly. "Call me if you need directions."

"Thank you, Benjamin." He turned to look at all of us. "I do hope I can be of some help."

The bell rang and we all started to run to our classes. "We'll see you tonight on-line!" Jenn shouted to Alex as she followed me inside.

As I walked back to class, I looked at Alex chatting comfortably with Bonnie. I couldn't understand why no one else seemed to be bothered by Alex. But then again, he was a new kid, and it couldn't hurt to be nice to the guy. I just hoped he wasn't going to lead us on a wild ghost chase.

# CHAPTER 5

The first thing I did when I got home late that afternoon was grab some cold lasagna from the refrigerator. Fortunately it was edible, although the noodles had the consistency of soggy cardboard. Grabbing a napkin, I headed into the study and dove into my homework. An hour later, I came up for air and turned on my computer, ready to tackle some investigative reporting.

As my modem connected me to the Internet, I thought about what I should look for first. Whenever I do research, I always begin by checking out a search engine on the World Wide Web. With hundreds of thousands of websites on the Internet, it's hard to figure out where to go first. A search engine does the work for you. You just have to type in what you're looking for, and then the engine spits out a list of places to go. The trouble with search engines is that you need to know what you're looking for in the first place. I typed the first thing that came to mind, Anthony T. Dragon+ghost, and hit Enter. One entry came up under the

*Somerset Weekly,* a newspaper that has been around since the gold rush in the mid-1800s. I read the following paragraph from an article dated October 10, 1907:

Anthony T. Dragon, Somerset's most mysterious resident, discovered the famous Yung Lo treasure after the San Francisco earthquake of 1906. Mr. Dragon, a miner, donated the treasure to the town last year with the provision that a new school and library be built, and a scholarship fund created. He has since disappeared without a trace, despite police and government efforts to locate him.

The town officially denies any of the rumors regarding ghosts or other mystical occurrences that surround this mysterious but generous man.

It wasn't much, but it was a start. I highlighted, cut, and pasted that paragraph into an e-mail and sent it to the rest of the gang. I printed out a copy for Alex, as well.

Curious about the article, I followed a link to the Yung Lo treasure at the website of the Fine Arts Museum of San Francisco, where it had recently been on display. The page outlining the history of the treasure read like a pirate adventure story. I could hardly believe it was real. The treasure had originally belonged to a Chinese emperor named Yung Lo in the 1300s. It was stolen by the emperor's cousin in 1403 and was never recovered. That is, until the San Francisco earthquake, when Anthony Dragon discovered the treasure and documents that told of the ship and the storms that carried it to the shores of California. Curious, I clicked on the link to look at the treasure.

There were silk tapestries that suggested complicated stories, colorful bowls carved with monkeys and other animals, and statues of laughing Buddhas and serious men with long mustaches. The most interesting item was the sculpture of a multicolored unicorn. Described as a "qilin," it had the body of a deer, the tail of an ox, horse's hooves, and a horn in the middle of its forehead. The inscription below said that the qilin was believed to bring good fortune to those who found it. "Interesting, but not what I'm looking for," I murmured. At least, that was what I thought at the time.

I got up to bring my plate into the kitchen just as my mom was coming in the front door. "Hi, honey." She kissed me on my forehead and handed me two big grocery bags. "Sorry I'm home so late, but it's been a crazy day." She took off her glasses, rubbed her eyes, and slumped into a kitchen chair.

"Boy, Mom, you look beat," I said. She really looked tired. Even her hair seemed exhausted, hanging in limp brown strands in front of her face instead of pulled back into her usual neat ponytail.

"I'm fine." She rested her chin in her hand and watched me unpack the groceries. "I think I'm teaching too many classes this semester. I thought it was hard to be a student, but it's nothing compared to creating lectures for three classes a week. I can't seem to keep up." She yawned, then got to her feet. "Let me finish with the groceries. You go on back to your work." She took the can of peas from my hand and gave me a gentle shove into the hallway. I walked back to the study and was just about to close the door when my mom called to me. "You have a good day?" she asked.

"Yup. Fine," I called. I couldn't tell her about what was going on in school. She had too many other things to worry about, and at this point there was nothing she could do to help me, anyway. I sat down at the desk and threw myself back into work. I had a half-hour to go before the seven o'clock chat, so I continued my search.

First I found a few articles on the web disproving the existence of ghosts, just to make myself feel better. I then tried to see if I could find a plan of the school posted anywhere. That would help us figure out how someone could get in without keys, and if any of the break-ins were connected.

I typed Somerset California+Maps into the search

engine. There were two entries: a current map of the town and a Chinese map of the Yung Lo treasure site. The map of the town looked standard, but I figured it might be useful, so I downloaded it and e-mailed it to Jenn to print out on her color printer. The treasure map was part of the museum exhibit pages. It was beautiful but confusing, much like a work of art in itself. As I was sending it to Jenn, I heard the doorbell ring.

I looked at the clock. 6:45. Alex was fifteen minutes early.

"I'll get it, Mom," I called out. "It's just someone from school." I went to the front door and opened it.

"Hello, Benjamin," Alex said, pushing his glasses up on his nose. "Thank you for having me to your house."

"No problem," I answered curtly. "Come on into the study." He followed me into the computer room. I pulled out the rolling desk chair next to mine and pushed it toward him.

Alex sat down and spun around on the chair. "You have a lot of books. Is your father a teacher?"

I turned back to the computer and said lightly, "I don't have a father. My mom works at the university, though." It took a lot of practice to be able to tell people that I never knew my dad, although it still didn't feel right inside when I talked about it.

My father left when I was just a few months old, and my mom never talks about him.

"Oh," was all Alex said. He got up and looked at the books, turning his head to one side to read the titles on the spines. I was glad he didn't ask any more questions about my family.

My mother told me that the polite thing to do when you ask a question and someone seems uncomfortable is to drop the subject. "Tact," she calls it. It was nice to know that Alex had tact, at least.

As I finished downloading the files, I gathered up the printouts I had just gotten off the web. "You may want to check out these articles," I suggested. "I e-mailed them to the others, so hopefully they'll read them by the time we start our meeting."

Alex walked over and took the printouts from me. "Thank you," he said as he started to look through them. "What does your mother do at the university?"

"She's a philosophy professor. She worked her way through college when I was a baby. She just finished her Ph.D., and this is her first year teaching full-time."

"You must be very proud of her. She must be very brave."

"Yeah. I guess she is," I said thoughtfully. I looked at my watch again. It was just about seven o'clock. "It's almost time for the others to arrive," I said, opening the chat room on the desktop.

"Are the others coming here, too?" Alex asked. "I thought we were going to meet on-line."

"We are meeting on-line, in our virtual conference room." A window appeared onscreen, revealing the room. "This is it," I said proudly.

"It is very cluttered," he said, wrinkling his nose.

"It started out as a photo of a newsroom that Fred scanned in from *Time* magazine," I explained. "But we added our own things to give it a more personal touch. When we use the room, we usually leave files for the others to drag to their desktops and take a look at. We're not always very good at cleaning them up when we're done."

Alex laughed. "Actually, it looks a lot like my room."

"Mine, too." I laughed with him, then suddenly realized something. "You need an avatar, Alex."

"A what?"

So, he doesn't know everything, I thought. "An avatar," I repeated. "It's an icon that you select to represent yourself on-line while you're chatting, so people can see who they're talking to."

"To whom."

"Huh?"

Alex rolled his eyes. "It's whom, not who. To whom they're talking."

"Whatever." This kid had to lighten up a bit if I was going to let him hang with me. I didn't care if he was the new kid in town. I turned back to the screen, pointing to my avatar. "I'm the Swiss cheese over here, because I'm the big cheese. Jenn, Fred, and Bonnie all picked avatars for themselves, too."

"What are they?"

Beep.

I looked up and saw the red queen standing in our virtual meeting room. "Perfect timing. That's Jenn," I explained to Alex.

I clicked on the cheese, then typed, Jenn. You're on time for once.

Words appeared under her avatar. Give me a break, Phillips. I'm not always late.

Beep.

A gray cat appeared onscreen next, followed by an image of a computer monitor with a curly brown mop of hair on top.

"Bonnie and Fred, yes?" Alex asked.

"You've got it. Now you have to choose yours." I turned to my other computer and opened my clip art folder. "Pick one from here," I said, as I sent a message on my PC telling the others to read the articles I had e-mailed.

"You must have hundreds of pictures here. How can I choose so quickly?"

"I have them organized by category. Sports, school, people, fictional characters, mythology, nature . . . What interests you? Just pick one quickly."

"It is a big responsibility to choose a character that represents you."

"Just choose something. It's no big deal," I urged, though from his expression I could tell that it was a big deal. Then I had an idea. In China, they have zodiac symbols that go by year, the way ours go by month. He could use his astrological sign. "What year were you born in? The year of the Rat, the Dragon, the Monkey? You can use that to represent you."

"That is an excellent idea. I was born in 1986, the year of the Tiger." He went through the folders until he found a tiger.

"Perfect." I copied it onto my PC. In a matter of seconds, the tiger showed up in the room next to the red queen.

Is that you, Alex? Jenn typed in.

"Now you have to respond," I told him. "Just click on your avatar, then type something in." I passed him the keyboard.

Yes. Hello, everyone. Nice room. Alex typed slowly, his fingers searching the keys for each letter. Then he handed the keyboard to me apologetically. "I am not a very good typist."

Ahhh. Do I detect a humble spot in Mr. Know-it-all's personality? I thought to myself. I took control of the keyboard and clicked on my cheese avatar so I could speak. Now that we're all here, let's get this meeting started, huh? I typed in quickly. I admit I was showing off a bit, but I couldn't help myself. Is everyone done reading the stuff I sent you?

Yup, Bonnie typed.

I'm done, too, Fred wrote.

Me three, typed Jenn. Nice tiger, Alex:)

"Why did Jenn use such strange punctuation at the end of her sentence?" Alex asked me.

"You mean the emoticon? That's for facial expressions," I explained. "If you turn your head to the left, it looks like a smiley face."

Alex turned his head to one side and studied it. "It has no nose," he said flatly.

"It's just a symbol, Alex."

BTW, I've got some bad news, you guys, Fred wrote.

"BTW?" Alex looked confused.

"Shorthand for 'by the way.' Like BRB is 'be right back,' and GG is 'gotta go,'" I explained to Alex.

What's the news, Fred? Bonnie asked.

I went by the pizza place after school, but someone had already claimed the keys. No one seemed to remember who picked them up.

That is bad news, Jenn responded.

Before I could add my comments, the screen winked out. "Whoa!" I hit the side of the monitor, thinking a connection was loose.

"What happened?" Alex asked, concerned.

"I'm not sure," I said, scratching my head. I got up and checked the connections, but everything was okay. The computer was still humming.

Just then, spooky music began to play through the speakers. A moment later, a picture of a skull appeared onscreen and laughed mockingly at us. Alex and I exchanged a surprised look. "At least you know your computer is not broken." Alex giggled nervously, trying to cut the tension.

But what showed up on the screen next made my mouth go dry.

BEWARE OF ANGERING THE DEAD. The scarlet letters scrolled out of the skull's mouth as blood-red droplets filled the screen. I jumped to the keyboard, typing every interrupt key combination I could think of without any luck.

Then, as suddenly as it appeared, the black screen winked out and we were back in the conference room.

It's okay, everyone, Fred typed. I flushed him out, whoever he was.

What happened? Bonnie asked.

There was a slight pause, then Fred wrote, You don't want to know.

Actually, we really do, I typed back.

How bad can it be? Jenn asked.

There was another pause, then Fred typed in, Someone was in the main computer room.

"Isn't the door locked?" Alex asked me.

"Anyone who found the keys would have access to the room." I gritted my teeth. Our worst fears had been realized.

Why couldn't someone honest have found the keys? I could almost hear Jenn whining as she typed.

All I know is I had a bear of a time kicking him or her off, Fred typed in.

It seems to me that we know only one person who is both good enough with computers and crafty enough to do something like this, Jenn wrote.

You mean Sly, don't you? Bonnie asked.

Alex looked confused. "Sly Wright? He is in my class, and he's a really bad student. How could he have done something this complicated?"

"He's a rotten kid and a bully," I said, "and he doesn't do too well in school, but he's definitely too smart for his own good."

"Or for our own good, for that matter." Alex was already counting himself as one of the team.

Wait a second, you guys. We're accusing Sly the way Thurdy and the others accused us. I hated to defend Sly, but I felt obligated to step in.

Just then another avatar appeared onscreen.

Incoming! Fred typed. Red alert!

I stared in amazement at the colorful unicorn. "It's a qilin," I said quietly.

Alex looked at me strangely. "How did you know that?"

"From Anthony Dragon's treasure," I answered. "There was a sculpture of one of these in the find," I said, gesturing to the screen. "But why would someone choose a qilin as their avatar?"

"It is usually an omen bringing good fortune to anyone who finds it." Alex stared at the screen for a moment before turning toward me. "Do you get strange visitors like this all the time?"

I laughed nervously. "I've always wished a big story would come and find me here in Somerset, but this is more excitement than I expected."

Do nOt B aFraid. Words appeared slowly below the qilin. i mean U no haRm. i M here 2 help.

This one's in the computer room, too. Fred typed quickly. I'm trying to disable the station without shutting down the whole system.

Sly, you dog-brained ratfink! Get off our system! Jenn certainly has a way with words when she's angry.

The mystery guest typed in sLy? No. I M not sLY.

Well, then, who are you and what do you want? Bonnie asked. And why did you come back?

i want 2 hELp U. This "guest" typed pretty slow-ly for someone who knew how to break into our conference room. There was SomEOne hERE B4. HE leFT.

I grabbed the keyboard. If this was Sly, then per-haps we could catch him in the act. What did this person look like?

He was tall and well-fed, had hair the color of dried straw, and had small spots on his face. The typing had improved in accuracy and speed.

"Not a flattering picture of Sly, or his freckles," I said to Alex.

"Would Sly say bad things about himself just to throw you off his track?" Alex asked thoughtfully.

"He's way too cocky for that." I thought for a sec-ond. "Are we thinking the same thing?"

"I think so," Alex said.

As I grabbed the keyboard to tell the others that it wasn't Sly, the qilin winked out of sight. Gotcha, Fred typed. He had just flushed out the interloper.

"Too late, Alex." I sighed, then broke the news to the others that the second person probably wasn't Sly.

At least we've got a lead on Sly, Jenn wrote.

Yes. But who was in the room after him? I typed. No one had an answer to my question.

# CHAPTER 6

"Can you believe it's still raining?" Fred came over to our table at lunch the next day, shaking the rain from his hair and jacket. He almost had to shout to be heard over the noise in the cafeteria. Just as it broke open, he dropped his wet lunch bag on the table. He caught the apple after one bounce on the floor, rubbed it on his shirt, and took a healthy bite.

"Yeah," I shouted back. "It's a good thing Jenn's dad left late this morning and gave us a ride, or we would have gotten soaked on the way to school."

"This is one time I am glad I take the bus to school," Alex said, sipping his milk. "The thunder and lightning started just after I left Benjamin's house last night. Unfortunately, I could not sleep for all the noise."

"Thunderstorms give me the creeps." Bonnie shuddered in front of her untouched veggie burger. "I was so scared last night, I ended up sleeping on the floor of my little brother's room!"

"You guys?" I tried to get the group's attention, but my voice was drowned out by a loud crack of thunder. After we coaxed Bonnie out from under the table, I tried again. "Listen, I've been thinking."

"Uh-oh," Jenn said under her breath.

I shot her a dirty look and continued. "We should probably check out the computer room for clues."

"Duh," Fred said sarcastically. "Even I realized that."

"We should check it out after school, I mean."

"You mean hang out in that dark basement after everyone's gone?" Bonnie asked, wide-eyed. "I have to be home by dinner time or my mom will ground me until next summer."

"We won't stay too late," I said. "We'll just wait until the after-school activities finish up. Then we'll look around and see if anything suspicious happens."

"Maybe we should set a trap for the culprit in case he or she comes back tonight," Jenn suggested.

"Hey, yeah! We could rig up a camera outside the computer room door," Fred suggested.

"But wouldn't someone see a camera?" I asked, taking a bite of my peanut butter-and-banana sandwich.

"Not the camera I have," Fred said, excitedly rummaging through his backpack and pulling out a tattered magazine page. "Check it out," he said, pointing out the features. "Remote control, digital, and totally wireless!"

"Cool! It must have cost you a fortune," I said, admiring the picture.

"Not a cent, man. It's Angelino's. He bought it as a security measure for the pizza place, and he wants me to make sure it works before installing it. This would be the best test of all."

"How would you mount it on the basement wall?" Alex asked, looking over Fred's shoulder.

"It's really light, so the bracket only needs one screw to hold it in place," Fred explained. "I figure we can put it up across the hall from the door, facing the entrance to the basement, so we can have advance warning in case anyone does show up."

"That actually sounds like a good plan." I was impressed.

"I guess that means we're staying after school, today, huh guys?" Jenn smiled as if daring any of us to object. No one said a thing. "Then it's settled. I've got the maps you found on the Internet in my desk. I'll bring them with me."

The five of us sat quietly in the dark on the floor of Bonnie and Alex's classroom, waiting for the last few meetings down the hall to finish up and the club members to go home. After that, there would just be Mr. Peabody, the security guard, making his rounds, and Sly and Thurdy alone in the detention room. At that point, we would all sneak off to the basement.

"You all get home safe now," Mr. Peabody called

to the kids in the chess club as they filed out the door. I listened as the front door clicked behind them and heard him mumbling to himself, "Yessiree. That's a nice bunch of kids." Mr. Peabody checked the door after them, then shuffled down the hallway toward the cafeteria, where I'd heard he usually spent most of the night."Oh my darlin', oh my darlin', oh my darlin' Clementine," he sang loudly as he walked. Mr. Peabody had been the night watchman at Dragon School for over forty years. He spent most of his time mumbling to himself and the rest of the time sleeping, from what I could tell. No wonder the school was having security problems.

I counted to ten after Mr. Peabody's footsteps had died away, then peeked through the small window in the classroom door.

Empty.

I opened the door with as little noise as possible and motioned to the other four to follow me. Our footsteps, though quiet, seemed to echo down the length of the hallway. My heart was beating so loud I was sure the others could hear it. We got to the basement door. Fred took out the keys with shaking hands, then steadied them as he turned the correct key in the lock. The five of us slipped through the door, letting it close behind us. We were in darkness. I flipped on the switch, flooding the basement with light.

"Everything looks a lot different when school's out, doesn't it?" Bonnie asked, her voice shaking.

Jenn squeezed her hand. "We're all here together, Bonnie. There's nothing to be afraid of."

"Yeah," Fred cracked, "Mr. Peabody is upstairs protecting us."

We walked down the long, narrow hallway to the computer room. Fred unlocked the door, and we all followed him in. I closed it behind us and turned on the light, breathing a sigh of relief. Jenn unrolled the printouts of the maps from the Internet and laid them out on the table in the center of the room. I double-checked the door to make sure we were securely locked in.

Fred sat down at the main computer terminal and started chuckling to himself as he typed away. Sitting down next to him, Jenn read over his shoulder and tried to keep from giggling.

"What's so funny, you guys?" Bonnie whispered.

Jenn pointed to the computer screen. Bonnie looked and stifled a laugh.

"What are you guys up to?" I asked, curious. Bonnie and Jenn were blocking my view so I couldn't see the screen. "You're not hacking into the school system are you?" I added, disapprovingly.

"Don't be such a stuffed shirt," Fred whispered back. "I'm just making some much needed improvements to the announcements for tomorrow."

"I feel bad for whichever kid is reading them tomorrow morning over the loudspeaker," Bonnie whispered. Then she let out a big hiccup. "'Scuse me. It's from trying not to laugh." She snorted, and Jenn started laughing harder.

While they were trying to hold each other up and stifle their giggles, I looked at the screen. For those students who choose to eat in the cafeteria, today's lunch is ratburgers and french flies. The school administration and the Board of Health, however, recommend eating at any of the nearby fast-food restaurants or your local dumpster, as the food will be both more nutritious and infinitely more flavorful. I tried not to laugh and suggested Fred change it back. "We don't want anyone to know we've been here tonight."

Fred rolled his eyes at me but dutifully changed it back. "It would have been really funny."

I unpacked the surveillance camera and held it in the palm of my hand. "There's no way anyone would notice this in a dark hallway," I said, impressed.

"Not if they weren't looking for it, anyway," Fred replied proudly. "We should be getting to work. Are you ready to roll?"

I nodded solemnly, handing him the toolbox and opening the door for him. As Bonnie followed Fred out, I gave her the flashlight and the camera.

"Do you guys need any help setting up?" I asked, hoping they'd say no.

"No problem," Bonnie said as she handed Fred a hammer.

"Just keep an eye on the monitor and let me know when an image shows up from the camera," Fred said.

"Will do." I closed the door behind me, relieved that I would be safely inside.

Jenn and Alex were peering closely at something on the table in front of one of the computers. "Look at this, Benji," Jenn called to me. "It looks as if our qilin guest from last night left us a present."

I came over and looked down at the sheet of paper she was pointing to. It was a blueprint labeled "Anthony T. Dragon School," with a tiny unicorn drawn in ink in the upper left-hand corner.

"What in the world . . ." I began.

"And here's the school on the town map." Jenn pulled out a printout of one of the two maps I had e-mailed her from my computer.

"That I could've figured out," I said impatiently. "But what does it have to do with the blueprint?"

"Just wait a second, Mr. Brainiac." She glared at me, then pulled out the treasure map. "Then here's the Chinese map to the Yung Lo treasure that Anthony Dragon found."

It was highly decorated, and the words were in

Chinese, but I could make out the locations pretty well. "This says that the dig site is over here." Alex pointed to the words next to an image of a white bird. I recognized the location as Carmen's Hill, a field on the edge of town.

"I knew that," I lied.

He raised his eyebrows at me but didn't respond, pushing his glasses up. "Now, if you compare the town map with the treasure map, you will see that the treasure map has a monkey where the school was built." He pointed to it.

"Maybe the school has some special meaning and that's why it's on the treasure map, too," I observed.

"There is also the matter of the symbols," Alex said, not bothering to respond. He pointed to the treasure map. "The white bird at the treasure site is a phoenix, which in popular Chinese mythology is associated with buried treasure. The monkey," he continued, pointing to the little creature on the school grounds, "is known as a trickster."

"Do you think there's something tricky about the school?" I asked, still not sure what I was looking at.

"Look," Jenn said, holding up the blueprint next to the treasure map. "The same monkey has been drawn on the plan of the school the qilin left us."

"And he's down in the basement—in the computer room," Alex said, sounding excited.

I looked closely at the monkey in the blueprint and then around me at the room. "This couldn't be the computer room," I said, pointing to the diagram. "There are two doors to the room in this diagram, but there's only one in here."

"Perhaps the monkey means we have been tricked," Alex said, pushing up his glasses. "Perhaps there is another door in this room, and perhaps it is hidden," he said ominously.

Suddenly, the door to the hallway opened and Fred and Bonnie rushed in. "Someone's coming!" Fred rasped in a harsh whisper as he quietly closed the door and locked it behind him. I panicked and jumped under the table. I felt better seeing Alex had done the same thing.

The jarring of the door caused the monitor to flicker and a dim view of the hallway came into view. "The camera is working!" Alex whispered.

I breathed a sigh of relief and said, "Not a moment too soon. Good job, you guys."

Bonnie crouched down next to me. "Um, Benji?" she said softly, her voice quivering with fright. "What do we do if it's someone dangerous?"

"Maybe it's just Mr. Peabody on his rounds," I suggested.

"Nah," Fred countered. "He's probably deep in dreamland."

"Shh." I could hear faint footsteps in the hall, and they were coming closer. "Turn out the light, Fred."

Fred got up silently and flicked off the light switch. It was completely dark except for the glow of the monitor. We all huddled on the floor and kept our eyes glued to the screen, waiting to see our visitor's face appear on camera. A dim shape came into view. The picture sharpened as it came closer to the door, the footsteps getting louder as they came near.

Sly's bulky figure was unmistakable. "I knew it," I whispered. Jenn shushed me.

We watched as he looked around to make sure he was alone. Then he pulled a ring of twenty or so keys from his pocket and fumbled to find the right one.

"Those are my keys, that weasel!" Fred whispered angrily as Sly fought with the door and impatiently tried each key in the lock.

"Excuse me, Fred, did you hit Record on the camera?" Alex reminded him.

"Dang!" Fred jumped up and hit the record button with the mouse. "Good call, Alex," he said over his shoulder.

"Did you get it, Fred?" Bonnie asked apprehensively.

Fred flicked off the monitor, then crouched back into his hiding position. "Got it. I also turned off the picture so Sly won't see he's being taped, when he finally comes in," he explained in a whisper.

"What do we do when he comes in?" Alex asked.

I didn't have any time to answer. Just then the key turned in the lock. A heartbeat later, Sly stepped into the room and switched on the light.

"Gotcha!" Fred shouted as he sprang for Sly, catching him off guard.

"Wha?" Sly toppled over backwards, but recovered quickly from his surprise. He caught at the door frame to keep from hitting the floor. Then he lunged for Fred, pushing him back into the room. Fred flew into the table, scattering maps and tools everywhere.

Sly stood in the door, panting. "So, you're back here tampering with the computers again, huh?" He straightened up, trying to get control of the situation. "Not a very smart thing to do with Thurdy and the police on your tails, is it?"

I stood up and stepped forward with more confidence than I felt. "Getting caught with those keys in your hand isn't very smart either," I pointed out.

"Yeah, well, nobody suspects me of anything," Sly said, crossing his arms smugly. "I've got nothing to worry about."

"Fat lot you know—" Bonnie started to say. I jabbed her in the ribs, and she had the sense to clam up. We didn't want Sly to realize he was being taped until we had a good confession out of him.

"You've got us there, Sly," I lied.

"I had a feeling you'd be smart enough to keep a set of keys, though, Phillips," he said to me. For some reason, I wasn't flattered. "But you weren't smart enough to plan ahead once you caught me." He rubbed his hands together like a cartoon villain.

"And you were smart enough to see this coming, I assume?" Jenn stepped forward, challenging him.

"As a matter of fact, I was. You forget there's a deadbolt outside the door," he said, backing out of the room. "I've got you guys trapped like rats in a maze. Vice Principal Thurdy will be very impressed with me once he hears what I've done."

"What, that you broke into the computer room and found us already here?" I had a hard time keeping the nervousness out of my voice.

"Not a problem, Benji Boy. I'll explain to him that I heard noises as I was leaving detention. I bravely came down to check things out and found you all here plotting with your maps and charts. Naturally I had to lock you in to make sure you'd still be here when I returned with him." Looking very impressed with himself, Sly grabbed the doorknob.

Fred rushed at him, but Sly slammed the door in his face, laughing wildly. We heard the padlock click shut. "Sit tight, kiddies!" he shouted through the door. "I'll be back soon to let you out." His laughter followed him down the hallway.

Fred banged on the door and rattled the knob, with no luck. "The lock is too strong. I can't break through." He sighed, leaning heavily against the frame.

"If we can't get out, we'll have to think of a good story for when Sly comes back with Thurdy," Jenn said, slumping into the only armchair in the room.

"If he comes back," I corrected her. "What's to stop him from leaving us here all night?"

I probably shouldn't have said that, judging from the look of panic that spread across everyone's face. The room fell silent as we all tried to figure out what to do.

"So we need a story in case he comes back with Thurdy," Jenn said thoughtfully. "But if he doesn't come back, we can't stay in here all night. I told my parents I'd be home by six-thirty. We have to find a way out."

"In a basement room with no windows? We would need some kind of magic to get us out of here." Fred rested his elbows on his knees and cradled his head in his hands.

"We do not need magic," Alex said quietly. He smoothed the basement blueprints out on the table. "We need a secret door."

"A what?" Fred jerked his head up in disbelief. "Where are you going to find a secret door?"

"He thinks he's found one on the map," I said, shrugging.

"Excellent!" Bonnie's eyes lit up as she leaned over to look at the plans with Alex.

Jenn shot me a look. "It's our only hope of getting out of here right now, so you'd better start believing it's here."

Jenn joined Alex and Bonnie in their huddle around the map as Fred and I examined the door seams for a way to break out of the room. After a few minutes of study, Alex came over to us. "It does not hurt to look, Benjamin. You need to examine all possibilities in a situation before discarding them, even something as unlikely as a secret door."

I hated admitting he was right. "Since we don't have anything better to do than sit here and wait, we might as well look around," I said reluctantly, then started handing out tasks. "We should probably check the whole room, just in case. Jenn and Alex, you check all four walls. Fred, check the mechanical stuff like the fuse box. Bonnie, you and I will look down here on the floor." Everyone scrambled to his or her assigned place, eager to be doing something instead of just sitting around waiting for Thurdy to appear.

After about five minutes, we had searched most of the room. I was feeling along the seam where the door frame met the floor, so I was the first to hear the faint footsteps. "They're coming!" I whispered. I looked up at the monitor, but no one was in view yet. "Anyone found signs of anything?"

A whispered chorus of "no" sank the last hope I had. Desperately I tried to come up with a good story, but realized that Thurdy would believe a gorilla like Sly before he would listen to anything we'd have to say.

"Hey, Fred," I whispered. "Save out a copy of our surveillance video, just in case."

"Good idea." Fred went over to the computer and clicked around with his mouse.

The footsteps were getting closer. I looked at the monitor and saw two dim shapes approaching the padlocked door. "We're in deep, you guys," I said, groaning. "Sly is coming with Thurdy."

"Keep looking," Jenn said, standing on the table, frantically checking the ceiling tiles.

They stopped just outside the door. Sly's muffled voice came through it: "I'm sure you'll be very interested in what's behind this door, Mr. Thurdy."

"This better be good, Orville," Mr. Thurdy said sternly.

I stood, my eyes frozen to the monitor, realizing there was no way out. I knew the secret door idea was a long shot, but I couldn't help being disappointed that it wasn't really there.

"Well, sir, this time you're going to be very impressed." Sly started to ramble on, building up the suspense for Thurdy and attempting to torture us in the process. I tuned him out, thankful, for once, for his tendency to gloat.

Just then, a click and the sound of sliding rock came from the corner. Alex was standing in shock in front of a floor-to-ceiling opening in the wall.

"You found it," Jenn whispered in awe.

We all clustered around the newly opened doorway, peering into the blackness. I was reminded of the red eyes I'd seen in the janitor's closet, but I didn't see them. Still, goosebumps rose on my skin.

"We've got to go in," I said quietly, looking back at the monitor. "Thurdy is taking out his keys, and we've only got a few seconds."

"But we don't know what's down there." Bonnie stared out into the blackness.

"It's got to be less trouble than we'll be facing in the next ten seconds if we stay," Jenn said.

"Wait! The disk!" Fred gasped, starting toward the computer.

"Leave it! We don't have the time!" I said and pulled him back, giving him a shove toward the entrance. The lock outside gave a loud click as we all threw ourselves into the opening and tumbled, head-over-heels, down a long chute to nowhere.

Behind us the passageway door closed magically, and we were left by ourselves in the darkness.

# CHAPTER 7

"Ow! Where are we?" Jenn looked up, blinking at the suddenly bright lights around us.

"I don't know. At least we had a soft landing, though." Bonnie got to her feet and dusted herself off.

"That is easy for you to say. You all landed on top of me," Alex said, groaning.

I pulled myself to my feet and helped the others up. "Is everyone okay?"

Jenn looked around. "It depends on where we are, I think."

We had landed in a well-furnished room with a high ceiling and one long, sofalike chair along one side of a table. "We're in a dining room," I said, as always, the master of the obvious.

"There are no chairs," Jenn said, looking under the table.

"It's sort of spooky, isn't it?" Bonnie said.

Looking around, I noticed the room was actually quite warm and comfortable—not at all what I expected to find underneath the school.

"I smell smoke," Bonnie said, sniffing. "Like a

fire in a fireplace with roasting chestnuts and mulled cider and . . ."

Jenn cut her off. "I smell it, too. I think it's coming from this way." She walked to a door opposite the one we came through, and we all followed closely behind her. When she opened the door, she stopped in her tracks, and we bumped up against each other like cars in a traffic jam.

The force of our bumping pushed us into the room, and we all stood still in shock. There, in the center of a spacious living room lined with shelves and shelves of books and a big fireplace, was what can only be described as a Chinese dragon. Not the paper kind that you see in a New Year's parade, mind you, but a living, breathing, real live dragon. It had the body of a serpent, twelve feet long, with shimmering blue-green scales and back claws like a lion's. His front half was even more frightening, with burning, red eyes and two cavernous nostrils. What I couldn't stop looking at, though, was his smile, a foot wide and filled with large, menacing teeth. He could eat all of us without batting an eye.

"Ahhhhhhhh!" was all I could get out.

"Ahhhhhhhh!" Fred and Bonnie screamed in unison.

The beast's smile grew wider, baring even more sharp teeth. "Visitors!" he exclaimed in a deep, rumbling voice, clapping his front paws gleefully. "Real live visitors."

"It's a monster!" Jenn yelled, hiding behind Fred. "Do something, Fred!"

"It's not a monster," Alex said, staring wide-eyed at the beast in front of us. "It's a Chinese dragon."

"Yes, I am. But don't be frightened," the dragon rumbled, still smiling. "I won't hurt you." As if to prove it, he shrank down, right in front of our eyes, until he was only about five feet long. The dragon cleared his throat. "Is that better?" he asked us uncertainly.

Bonnie screamed again.

"Is that all she can do?" The dragon turned to Alex, his voice soft but booming, like a late-night radio announcer's.

"I think she is in a bit of shock, Mr. Dragon, sir," Alex explained. "And I cannot say that I blame her," he added, taking a step back.

"I am so sorry," the dragon said humbly. "Where are my manners? You're the first guests I've ever had. How could I be so impolite?" He walked up to us and bowed deeply. "Allow me to introduce myself. You can call me A.T."

"It's nice to meet you, A.T., " Jenn said, bowing just as formally. "My name is Jenn." She introduced the rest of us, and we each bowed in turn. "Allow me to introduce you to Benji, Alex, Bonnie, and Fred."

"It's a pleasure," the dragon said, smiling awkwardly. Despite his teeth and claws, his childlike glee made him quite likable. Becoming a little more relaxed, I could almost forget that he could swallow us whole if we turned our backs for a moment.

Feeling brave, I reached out and offered my hand for him to shake. He tilted his head sideways as if he was trying to figure out what to do, then he grasped my hand gingerly in his paw. His skin was hard and smooth, like a lobster shell, and not slimy at all, as I had expected. "Oh!" he exclaimed with surprise. "I thought humans would be a lot mushier. You're actually pretty solid."

I laughed, realizing that he was just as wary of us as we were of him.

"I'm afraid I have no seats to offer you, but please take some cushions from over there and have a seat on the floor," the dragon said.

While we were standing there nervously looking at each other, the dragon walked back to a long couch, much like the one in the other room, and did the most incredible thing I had ever seen. First he took a deep breath as if he were inflating a balloon inside his chest, which made his whole body rise three feet. Then, he floated over to the sofa, let out all his air, and sank into the plush fabric. He looked at us impatiently and again suggested we sit.

I shrugged my shoulders and picked up a plush,

red velvet cushion from the corner of the room. Plopping it down on the floor, I looked up expectantly at the others. One by one, they did the same, grabbing overstuffed pillows and clustering in front of the dragon.

"That's better." The dragon sighed. "You were beginning to make me nervous."

I laughed uncomfortably. "We were making you nervous?"

"I guess this is new to all of us, isn't it?" He laughed. "Well, I promise not to eat you if you don't run off and tell on me," he said, smiling. "Is it a deal?"

"Eat us?" Bonnie exclaimed, panic-stricken.

"He's joking, Bonnie," Jenn reassured her, then looked up at the dragon. "Aren't you?"

"Of course!" The dragon plucked an apple out of the basket beside his couch, threw the entire thing into his mouth and closed it with a loud crunch and gulp. "I'm a vegetarian." He licked his lips with his long, forked tongue.

"You're a vegetarian?" Bonnie brightened. "Me, too."

That seemed to break the tension a bit. At least, enough for all of us to start asking questions at once.

"So what exactly are you doing down here, A.T.?" I asked.

"And for how long?" Jenn asked.

"Where did you come from?" Alex chimed in.

"Are there any more of you?" Fred asked cautiously.

"Are you a vegetarian for ethical or for health reasons?" Bonnie asked.

"Whoa! Too many questions at once!" The dragon held up his front claws in protest. "Perhaps it will be easier if I tell you who I really am." He shifted in his seat and cleared his throat. "I am Anthony, the Dragon."

"Anthony, the Dragon?" I repeated softly. "As in Anthony T. Dragon?" I asked in awe.

"One and the same." The dragon straightened up proudly.

"But Anthony T. Dragon was a gold miner . . ." Fred began.

"And he's most certainly dead by now . . ." Jenn continued.

"And he's not a dragon!" I managed to spit out.

The dragon sighed and said, "That is what I had to lead everyone to believe. But I just had to make up that story to protect myself."

"Protect yourself?" Bonnie finally managed to stammer.

The dragon turned to look at Bonnie. "Protect myself," he repeated. "What would you have done if you got a note saying 'Hello, I'm Anthony, the

Dragon, and I have this treasure I've been guarding for five hundred years that I'd like to give you. Don't bother trying to find me, though, because I'd really rather remain anonymous, thank you very much'?" He looked at us questioningly, but we were all too stunned to answer.

"Well, I'll tell you," he continued. "People would come hunting for more treasure and end up destroying my house in the process. And then others would come hunting for me instead, and I'd end up being poked and prodded by scientists in some laboratory."

"So you made up the story of the miner to throw people off your track."

"Precisely, Alex."

I stood there staring in disbelief, trying to comprehend that what I was looking at was a five-hundred-year-old, real live dragon. I had so many questions, I didn't know what to ask first.

"So why did you donate the treasure to the town?" Jenn asked, beating me to it.

A.T. smiled. "It is a long story," he said, jumping off the sofa with a light thud and standing directly in front of us as though he were center stage. "A long time ago, back in China, I belonged to an emperor named Yung Lo. He kept me hidden away among his treasures," he explained, "and allowed me out only to entertain his guests with my magic.

One day, the emperor's cousin and his small army of men snuck into the storeroom of the palace, gathered up the treasures—myself among them—and sailed with them out to sea before anyone even got to sound an alarm.

"We should have been caught right away. However, as luck would have it, a storm carried us off course, and we drifted out into the ocean. Many months later, we came to the shore of what is now San Francisco.

"It became my duty to guard the treasure against any attacks. Eventually, the men all died, and I was left alone in my cave. I sat guarding the Yung Lo treasure for hundreds of years until I realized that I had become obsolete. I mean, no one needed me to guard a treasure that people had forgotten four hundred years before. In your world, there is a name for people who hoard up all their gold, get no pleasure from life, and give nothing to anyone else. I was not a brave dragon, I was a miser," he said, hanging his head in shame. When he looked up at us, the usual sparkle returned to his eyes. "Once I realized that, there was only one thing left for me to do."

"What was that?" Bonnie asked.

"I donated the gold to the town so that they could sell the treasure and build a school. I figured the treasure would be better preserved in a museum than in a dusty, old cave," the dragon said, smiling.

"So how did you keep yourself hidden?" Jenn asked.

A.T. chuckled. "I made a Chinese treasure map, marked the treasure site with a white phoenix, and sent the map to the Somerset mayor's office. In the accompanying letter, I said that the treasure was to be used to build a school and a library. I signed it 'Anthony T. Dragon, miner.'"

"How about the monkey?" I asked. I still couldn't fit the whole story together.

"That was my own private joke," the dragon answered. "I left a clue to my true home just in case anyone was determined enough, or clever enough, to find me. No one ever has been, of course—until now, that is." His red eyes beamed at us. "No one in town ever caught sight of Anthony T. Dragon the miner, but my instructions were carried out to the letter. That's why the school was built above my tunnel, so I could visit whenever I wanted to."

"And you built the secret door in the basement?" Bonnie asked.

"That's right, though I haven't used it all that often." A.T. leaned on the mantel of the fireplace. "A few years after the school was built, I went into hibernation for a while," he said, rubbing his eyes. "I wake up about once every twenty years. In fact, I just woke up a couple of weeks ago."

Suddenly a thought crossed my mind as I put the facts together. "When you woke up, did you start visiting the school at night?"

"Yes, I did." He picked up a book from the mantel and held it out to show us. It was from the school library. "I've been catching up on my reading."

"So that's what's been happening," I said slowly as the truth dawned on me.

Alex nodded his head as if he shared the same thought. "I believe you are correct, Benjamin," he said, smiling.

"What are you guys talking about?" Bonnie whined.

Jenn smiled as though she understood as well. "A.T. is the one who has been visiting the school at night."

"You mean he was the one who knocked over the shelves in the library?" Bonnie asked.

The dragon looked embarrassed. "I guess I did that with my tail." It almost looked like he was blushing. "That was before I figured out how to change size." He grew a few inches and then shrank back down again as if to demonstrate. "Five hundred is young for a dragon, and I am discovering new talents all the time," he explained.

"So you crashed the main computer, too." Fred pointed an accusing finger at A.T.

"Oh, no. That wasn't me." The dragon held up his claws in protest.

"Then it must have been Sly," I concluded.

"I'm sorry to say I didn't see who it was," the dragon apologized.

"But what about the other stuff that happened?" Fred asked. "Who took the food from the cafeteria and who broke in on our chat session?"

"Perhaps I can explain, Fred," A.T. said, coming forward. "When I woke up, I was ravenously hungry. The first thing I did was follow the smell of food." He walked over to a box on the side of the room, lifted the lid, then took out a granola bar and sniffed it. "This was the only thing in the food room that smelled edible, so I took a few to tide me over until I figured out where else to forage for food." He looked at the granola bar and popped it in his mouth, wrapper and all. "Mmmmm!" He rolled his eyes and happily patted his stomach. "I must say, these granola bars taste much better than they did back in the 1970s."

"What about the other night in the chat room?" I asked.

"Well, last night that well-fed spotted boy came in and made the computer do all sorts of horrible things, then he finally left, using very foul language. I watched him at the keyboard and followed the same steps to make the picture appear on the screen."

"So it was you last night!" Alex said happily. "You were the unicorn."

"You must be a very quick study." Fred looked impressed.

The dragon seemed to blush. "I remember things after I've seen them done once or twice," he said modestly.

"Why did you leave us a map of the secret door so we could find you?" Bonnie asked, looking at the dragon intently. "I mean, you did want us to find you, didn't you?"

A.T. looked shy. "Five hundred years is a long time to go without talking to someone," he explained, "and you seemed like such interesting children. Besides," he said with sudden energy, "I would like to help you catch this Sly person. I don't like him, and I certainly don't like the fact that he's getting all of you in trouble."

Jenn turned to me, laughing. "A.T. certainly is a good judge of character," she said.

"Why thank you, Jenn." The dragon bowed slightly.

Alex looked at his watch. "Right now what we need is a way to get home quickly. It is almost six."

The dragon clapped his hands excitedly. "I can certainly help you with that!" He walked to a side door and opened it. "Follow me and I'll have you home in no time!"

# CHAPTER 8

We followed A.T. through a labyrinth of passage-
ways covered with overstocked bookshelves. I
whistled appreciatively. "You've got more books
than the Somerset Library!"

"I don't get out much, so I spend a lot of time
reading," A.T. said over his shoulder. "I've been
asleep for quite a while, so I have a lot of catching
up to do. I hear some great things have been written
in the past twenty years." He slithered quickly
down the corridor, and we followed close behind.

Finally, after a few minutes that felt like forever, he
turned a corner and started up a long sloping hallway.
"This way." He turned to us, beckoning with his claw.
We all looked at each other curiously, with no idea of
where he was taking us.

When we reached a door, A.T. opened it, and we
all gasped in surprise. We were at the edge of town
on top of a hill. There wasn't a cloud in the sky, and
the stars were shining almost as bright as the lights
of the town below us.

"It's beautiful up here," Bonnie said, sighing.

Jenn clung to the mouth of the cave, cautiously
leaning out to take a look. "We're a bit high up for

my liking." She shivered, although only a light, fall breeze was blowing.

"Don't be afraid, Jenn," the dragon said soothingly as he swiveled his neck to talk to her. He turned his head and the rest of him followed gracefully, in one fluid movement. "Come see. It's wonderful up here." He took her hand gently in his claw and guided her away from the cave. "As long as I am nearby, nothing bad can happen to you. It's part of my magic."

Jenn still looked skeptical but stood more comfortably at the edge of the hill.

A.T.'s eyes were shining. He looked as excited as a child at a birthday party. "Watch." He lay down flat on his stomach and stretched out like a log. There were popping and stretching sounds as he inflated to about twelve feet long. All at once, five scales on his back separated and stood straight up, forming five rounded seat backs. "Climb on!" he said to us excitedly.

I looked at him, not understanding. "What for?"

"I can take you all home," he answered. "Please, get on."

"You can fly?" I asked, awestruck.

A.T. nodded happily.

"But you don't have any wings," Bonnie said.

"Don't need 'em," the dragon replied. "This is one of my magical talents I've been practicing for centuries. Be assured, it is safe."

"Wow!" Fred exclaimed as he grabbed hold of a scale on the dragon's back and scrambled into one of the makeshift seats.

Bonnie climbed up next. "This is incredible!"

Alex cautiously eyed the other two already up on the dragon's back, strapping themselves in with the seat belts that appeared when the scales lifted. "Dragons do not lie, so as long as you tell me no harm can come to me . . ." He didn't finish his sentence but climbed into the front seat on the dragon's back and strapped himself in.

I really wanted to go up and take one of the two remaining seats, but I didn't want to leave Jenn standing there alone. "Jenn?" I looked at her questioningly. "Are you coming?"

She looked like she was about to shake her head no, then said, "Why not?" She climbed into the third seat, leaving the second one for me.

I grabbed onto the seat back and found it was remarkably easy to swing my leg up and over into a comfortable sitting position. I strapped myself in tightly and checked it twice despite what A.T. said about his magic protecting us. Just in case, I thought.

"Is everybody ready?" A.T. asked.

"Our seat backs are up and our tray tables are in their locked and upright positions," Bonnie said, mimicking the flight attendants she must have heard on an airplane.

"Well, then we're off," A.T. said as we lifted weightlessly off the ground and hovered there for a moment. "Hold on," he said, and we slid gently into the night air.

I've been in airplanes before, and they're okay for getting you from place to place. But let me tell you, for sheer enjoyment, flying by dragon is the only way to go. A.T. took off and flew as though he were swimming underwater. His body slithered through the air like a snake through water. Serpentine. The word flashed through my mind as I connected it to the dragon's movements.

We were stunned to silence as we climbed even higher above the town, each of us peeking cautiously over the side at first, then becoming more daring as we were distracted by the landmarks below.

Jenn leaned forward and whispered to me, "I'm still afraid to open my eyes."

"There's nothing to it, Jenn," I shouted back to her. "You've got to see how cool this is. It's a once-in-a-lifetime experience!"

"You're right," she said shakily. "If none of you are nervous, there's no reason for me to be such a scaredy cat." She put her hand on my back. "Okay. Here goes."

She must have opened her eyes just then, because I heard her gasp and her hand dropped from my shoulder. I turned around in my seat to see what had happened. She was looking up, open-mouthed, at the stars above. "I never knew it was so beautiful up here," she whispered in awe.

"I'm glad you're enjoying it so far, but it's getting late and I haven't even shown you the best part." A.T. looked back at each of us in turn. "Are your seat belts fastened securely?"

We each checked our seat belts and told him we were all set.

"Well, then." He smiled back at us mischievously. "Hold on tight!"

With that, he picked up speed until he caught an air current and swooped straight up.

"Agghhhh!" We all screamed as we found ourselves going through a backward loop. My stomach followed, not seeming to be able to keep up with the dragon's flight.

We caught another air current and went into a second loop. "Wheee!" I heard Jenn squeal with delight behind me as all of us, including A.T., broke into laughter.

"One more time?" A.T. asked.

"Yes!" Jenn shouted back. We all laughed even harder and echoed her agreement.

The next flip was the highest yet. I clung to the seat belt and tried not to close my eyes, although I was tempted.

"This is better than the loop-de-loop at Great

Mountain!" Fred exclaimed after A.T. had slowed down to a comfortable cruising speed.

"Again!" Bonnie shouted.

A.T. shook his head. "Sorry, my friend. It's time I fulfilled my first promise and got you all home."

"How are you going to get us home without being seen?" I asked.

"Actually, one of my favorite games to play is hide-and-seek," the dragon admitted.

"Hide-and-seek?" Bonnie asked.

"Yes. People see only what they want to see—only what they can understand. I've stood right in front of Principal Mullins, quite by accident, mind you, and he didn't see me at all!"

"That's what I was trying to tell Benjamin yesterday!" said Alex. "You need to believe in something before you see it."

I kept my mouth shut. Just the day before I chose to believe I was going crazy when I saw those red eyes, rather than admitting to seeing A.T. right in front of me. "For someone who claims to be a good newsman, I'm not always that good at keeping an open mind, I guess," I finally admitted.

"So whom do I drop off first?" A.T. changed the subject and turned to give me a secret wink as though he understood what I was thinking.

"I live just a couple of blocks away. Over to the left," Bonnie said, pointing right.

"Which left do you mean?" the dragon asked, stifling a laugh.

"That way," Bonnie said, pointing right again but sounding definite.

"That would be your right, Bonnie," Jenn said, gently.

"It's from being on her head too much," I said, laughing. "Everything is backward."

A.T. said nothing as he took off in the direction Bonnie had indicated. He has tact, too, I thought.

"It's the first house at the end of the block," Jenn said.

The dragon landed on her front lawn as a car drove by and slowed down. Oh no, I thought. Someone's going to see A.T., and it'll be all over!

The car horn honked and the driver's side window was rolled down. "Hi, Bonnie!" a woman said out the window. "Tell your mom to give me a call!" Bonnie waved back as the woman rolled up the window and drove off.

The dragon gave us a satisfied smile. "See what I told you? Fun, isn't it?"

We all looked at each other and laughed, not believing what we had just seen, or rather, what that woman had clearly missed. I don't want to become a grown-up like that, I thought to myself, then I realized that until just a few hours before, that was exactly what I was on my way to becoming.

# CHAPTER 9

The next morning, when I walked out of the house, Jenn was waiting impatiently on my front stoop. "You're on time, for once!" I exclaimed.

She sprang up from the step and bounded over to me. "I couldn't sleep a wink all night! I kept thinking about A.T. and how exciting everything is. I've pinched myself so much to make sure I'm not dreaming that I think I'm black-and-blue." She rubbed her forearm.

"Yeah, well, you never were the brightest light bulb in the chandelier," I said, then ducked to avoid her fist. "I was only kidding."

"Aren't you excited about all this, Benji?" she asked as we started off down the street.

I thought for a moment, then answered her. "I guess so. It's really neat, finding A.T. I mean, how many kids get to meet a real live dragon and don't get eaten by him in the first five minutes?"

"A.T. is a vegetarian," Jenn pointed out.

"True," I said. "He's full of surprises. But I think we can trust him."

"We've got A.T. on our side now," Jenn agreed.

"But we've still got to prove to Thurdy and

Mullins that they're barking up the wrong tree. We didn't mess up the computer system. Sly's the one they should be after. If only we had taken a copy of the video." I picked up a rock and threw it at a near-by tree. It bounced off the tree and into a bush.

"Ouch!" A gruff voice grumbled from the bush as the leaves began to rustle.

Jenn and I looked at each other quizzically. "Um, hello?" I peered in through the leaves and saw A.T. rubbing his head and sulking.

"Why did you have to throw it so hard?" A.T. whined.

"I'm sorry, A.T. I didn't know you were hiding in there," I apologized.

Jenn leaned into the bush. "Hi, A.T.! What are you doing in there?"

"Oh, I'm just hanging around. I've decided to do some snooping of my own. It looks like so much fun when you guys do it." He rubbed his head again. "Perhaps next time I'll bring some armor."

Fred skated up behind us. "Hey, Benji. Talking to the shrubbery again?"

"No, not the shrubbery," I replied. "Fred's here, A.T.," I spoke into the bush.

The dragon popped up like a jack-in-the-box, said "Hello, Fred," then ducked back down just as quickly.

"Hey, A.T. Good thing you're in there. I thought

these guys were going batty." Fred hopped off the skateboard and peered into the bush. "I'm actually glad you're here, because I've been thinking."

"Really?" I said. "I'm impressed."

Ignoring my sarcasm, Fred continued earnestly, "Even if we can nail Sly for all the bad stuff he did, we can't pin the missing food or the toppled bookshelves on him."

"You've got a point," Jenn said. "That's all stuff that A.T. did. No offense, A.T."

The dragon's long mustaches drooped, and he looked down sadly. "I didn't mean to get you guys in trouble."

"We know that, A.T. But we do need a cover story for you," I replied gently.

"Well, I can give back the granola bars I haven't eaten," he suggested.

"And we can pool our money to replace the rest, and tell them we found the cases behind the school," Fred suggested.

"But what about the toppled bookshelves in the library?" Jenn asked.

"Hmmm." Fred appeared deep in thought. None of us said anything for fear of breaking his concentration. "Minor seismic activity," he said finally.

"What?" the three of us said together.

"Small earthquakes that are so insignificant they don't get reported in the news. It happens often enough out here in Northern California that it wouldn't seem weird. I can tell them I found out about it on a website. All it takes is one shelf to topple, and the rest fall like dominoes, anyway. As long as they don't check up on our story, we'll be fine."

I was about to reply when a voice came from behind us. "If you're looking for your keys, I can guarantee they're not in those bushes." I wheeled around to see Sly standing on the sidewalk, looking angry. "I don't know how you guys managed to get out of that room last night, but if there's one thing I hate, it's when people make me look bad!"

"You do a good job of that all by yourself, Orville," A.T. commented from his hiding place.

"Hey! Which one of you said that?" Sly demanded, hands on his hips.

"Said what?" Fred replied innocently.

"Tell me, Sly," I rushed in to call his attention away from the bush. "What were you doing in the computer room last night, anyway?"

Sly stood over me and breathed down my neck. "I don't have to answer to you, shrimp-boy!"

As I stood there cowering, the bush rustled and A.T. gave a deep growl. Sly jumped back and yelped, and Jenn walked over and poked him in the chest. "If you don't want to know what we've got hiding in that bush, you'd better answer the question, Sly."

Sly's eyes widened as he looked at the shaking and growling bush. A.T. let out a low howl and Sly jumped back, saying, "Nice doggie—or whatever you are." He pleaded with us. "I'll tell you guys whatever you want, just don't let it get me!"

It took all I had to keep from giggling. A.T. was really doing a great job. We couldn't have planned it better if we had tried, I thought to myself. I straightened up and tried to look stern. "So, Sly, why are you trying to frame us?"

"Wait a sec," Jenn said, rummaging through her backpack. I heard a click, but her hand came out of the bag with a fresh wad of bubble gum. She stuck it in her mouth and started chewing. "Okay. Now we're ready to listen." I could tell she was up to something, but I couldn't imagine what it was.

"Look," Sly said, licking his lips nervously. "I wasn't trying to frame anyone. When I found out about the trouble you guys got in when the system crashed, I just wanted to see you get what was coming to you. Then I heard you guys talking in the hall on Monday about the missing keys. I figured finding them would help me get Thurdy to catch you guys in the act. I hate being the only one who gets caught all the time." He pointed his finger at me. "I bet you do bad stuff all the time, Phillips. But do you ever get caught? No way. I'm the one who's on permanent detention."

"Hold on. You mean to tell us that you didn't get the keys until Monday?" I asked.

"I didn't know anything about it until you blurted it out in the hallway," Sly replied.

Jenn, Fred, and I exchanged confused looks. "If you didn't get the keys until Monday, how did you get in over the weekend to erase the grades?" Jenn asked him.

Sly held his hands up. "Oh no. You can't pin that on me. I'm not getting in trouble for something you guys did." He actually looked like he was telling the truth. "I admit I had fun using the keys the other night. You must have really freaked out when I hacked into your chat room." He snickered, and A.T. growled more deeply. Sly pointed a finger at the shaking bush. "Now, call off your dog, or whatever that foul-smelling menace is." A.T. jumped out of the bush with a roar, eyes blazing and jaws wide open.

"Mommy!" Sly screamed and took off down the street as the four of us stood there laughing.

"Thanks, A.T.!" I said, holding my sides from laughing so hard. "You were great. I only wish we had some evidence of what Sly said."

Jenn grinned and dug into her backpack. "Actually, we do." She held up a mini tape recorder and pressed stop. "I recorded the whole thing!"

"Smart thinking, Jennifer!" A.T. patted her on

the back. "I've got a lot to learn from you all." He shook his head in awe.

Suddenly something from the conversation dawned on me. "You know what this means, don't you?" I asked them, grinning broadly.

"Not really." Fred looked up at me blankly.

"Think about it. If you have an alibi from Angelino that you lost the keys on Friday at the Pizza Zone, and Angelino can also admit that some one picked up the keys on Monday, it gets us all off the hook!" I said triumphantly.

"You're right!" Jenn jumped up and hugged each of us in turn. "We're in the clear!"

Fred smiled. "This is great!" Then his face dropped. "That is, as long as they don't find out we had an extra set of keys."

"I guess we can't use the surveillance video we left in the computer room as evidence, now," Jenn sighed.

"Yeah, but thanks to you we have a taped confession that doesn't mention the fact that we were there last night," I reassured them. "They'll never need to know we had those other keys."

"You know," A.T. said, his face screwed up in concentration, "it still doesn't tell us who destroyed the system."

"But at least they'll know it wasn't us," I pointed out. "We need to tell Principal Mullins right away."

"Tell him what?" Bonnie asked. She and Alex came up behind us.

A.T. popped up from the bush and announced, "We're off the hook!"

Bonnie squeaked, and she and Alex jumped back in surprise.

"What do you mean 'off the hook'?" Bonnie asked.

"We got a taped confession from Sly that proves none of us could have broken into the computer room on Saturday," Jenn explained in a rush.

Bonnie and Alex looked confused. "How did you manage that?" Alex asked, surprised.

"I'll explain it to you on the way to the office," I said, turning to walk toward the school. The others followed me, almost forgetting A.T.

A.T. crouched in the bush, looking sad. "What about me?"

"Poor A.T." Bonnie reached into the branches and patted him on the head. "I think you'll have to miss out on the fun this time."

His mustaches drooped again and he hung his head, then suddenly he perked up. "I know! If I can make myself small enough, then I can fit in one of your knapsacks." He proved this by shrinking down to about two feet long. Then he coiled himself up like a rope, looked up at us, and smiled innocently. "I promise not to growl at anyone," he said.

I took out my books and handed them to Fred, then held the bag open for the dragon. "Climb in, A.T." I hoped he wasn't too heavy.

A.T. slithered into the bag. "Just leave it open enough for me to breathe. And to hear what's going on."

I zipped it halfway and hefted the bag onto my shoulder. I felt him shifting around on my back. Luckily he was pretty light, but I hoped he would settle down. "How are you doing back there?" I asked.

"Just peachy" was the dragon's muffled reply.

As we walked into the building, Thurdy eyed us suspiciously with his slit eyes. When we reached the principal's office, Miss Trumbull, Principal Mullins's assistant, showed us right in. "He asked me to call you all in later this morning, but since you're here now, you might as well go in."

As we walked in the door, Principal Mullins greeted us warmly. "Come in. Come in." He motioned for us to sit down. I placed the bag with A.T. in it beside my chair and opened the zipper a little so the dragon could hear. "I'm glad you all stopped by," the principal said. "How is everything going?" He looked concerned.

"Actually, we have some news," Jenn told him, smiling.

The principal raised his eyebrows. "Good news, I hope. What have you found?"

"We've been doing some investigating," I began, then told him our story about the granola bars and the minor earthquakes. He seemed skeptical but luckily didn't challenge us.

After I finished telling the story, I told him about Sly's taped confession. Jenn opened her bag, took out the tape recorder and played the tape for the principal. Bonnie giggled when she heard A.T.'s growl on tape. Fred poked her in the ribs and she straightened up, but not before she began to hiccup. "'Scuse me," she said quietly.

When the tape ended, the principal rested his fingers on his chin and was quiet for a moment. Finally he said, "This is all very interesting, and quite incriminating for Orville, but unfortunately it seems to bring up more mysteries than it solves."

I looked at him questioningly. "What do you mean, sir?"

"What missing keys was Orville talking about?" he asked.

Fred's face reddened. "Um . . . I think I should answer that. I left them at Angelino's on Friday when I was helping him install a pinball machine. Sly got them on Monday, claiming to be picking them up for me."

The principal looked at Fred sternly. "That was very irresponsible of you to lose those keys, Fred." Then he sat back with a hint of a smile on his face.

"If Angelino can confirm your story, however, you kids have proven your innocence."

From inside my bag, A.T. started to applaud. I coughed and moved my chair to drown out the noise.

Principal Mullins tapped his chin with his forefinger, frowning. "Once we get those keys back from Orville, I'm afraid I'll have to keep them. Mr. Thurdy might have been right. I may be giving you kids more responsibility than you can handle."

I stifled a groan and was about to protest when Alex motioned toward the door. I turned around and saw Thurdy the Night Creature standing there with an evil grin on his face. "I'm glad you came to your senses, Mullins," he said with a smirk. "You shouldn't have given them those keys in the first place. They pose a real security risk."

"You may be correct, but I believe this is just one new security measure that needs to be taken in this school," the principal answered him.

"What exactly do you propose?" Thurdy asked. I thought I detected a note of panic in his voice.

"Well, I think we should have an alarm system installed as well as security cameras placed around the school," the principal replied. "And perhaps Mr. Peabody might need an assistant. He seems to be finding the job a bit tiring lately."

Thurdy hesitated for a moment with a calculating look on his face, as though he was weighing his options. When he finally spoke, his voice had become slick, almost oily. "You're right about Peabody, obviously. He's constantly asleep on the job. Just last Saturday night, I found him sleeping on the couch in the basement. We have no way of knowing what he is up to when no one is around."

As Mr. Mullins began to talk about his plans for revamping security, a thought suddenly struck me. "Mr. Mullins?" They both turned to look at me. "Excuse me for interrupting, but did Mr. Thurdy just say he was here in the school on Saturday night, the night of the computer hack-in?"

The Night Creature turned even paler than usual and began to sputter. Mr. Mullins looked quizzically at Thurdy. "You did just say that, didn't you, Tyron?"

"Well, yes," he replied, as if searching for words. "Actually I was here early in the evening. I . . . um . . . was going to a dinner party and realized I had left my overcoat in the office. I came in and went out directly."

"Oh. I see," said the principal.

Just then the door opened and Miss Trumbull walked in. "Excuse me, Mr. Principal, but the president of the school board is here to see you."

Mr. Mullins stood up and walked to the door. "You can send her in, Miss Trumbull. And see that these students get notes for their teachers," he said. Then he turned to us as we stood up. "You all did a fine job. I'm very proud of all of you. It won't be long now before we find the real culprit."

We walked out into the empty hallway with Thurdy close behind us. As the principal closed the door, Thurdy wheeled around and demanded, "What did he mean by that last comment?"

"Oh, didn't you hear?" Jenn said sweetly. "We're in the clear. We've got an alibi."

"That's impossible," Thurdy spat out.

"No, actually it is not impossible at all," Alex said. "In fact, it is quite possible that we know who did it, although we do not have any proof." Alex then added, "At least, not yet."

Thurdy didn't answer, but just stared wide-eyed. I wasn't sure what Alex was up to.

"Why were you in the basement on Saturday night? You would have found your overcoat in your office, Mr. Thurdy, but you said you saw Mr. Peabody sleeping on the couch in the basement," Alex said pointedly.

So that's it, I thought. Good going, Alex. I studied Thurdy, waiting for his response. Thurdy looked around the hallway wildly, like a trapped raccoon, but he didn't say anything. Everyone grew very still.

I leaned toward Thurdy and looked him in the eye. "You went into the computer room, didn't you?"

"You can't prove anything." The Night Creature looked at us venomously. "I won't have you pinning things on me. You're just a bunch of kids. I'm the vice principal!" He realized he was almost shouting. He lowered his voice to a harsh whisper. "But at least one good thing came of all this. You got your wings clipped by Mullins taking away your keys. Now you can't go snooping into other people's affairs." With that, he turned on his heel and stormed away, mumbling to himself. I thought I caught the phrase "could have ruined everything," but that might have been my imagination.

We all looked at each other, dumbfounded.

Finally, I broke the silence. "So it must have been Thurdy who crashed the computers after all," I said. "But why would a vice principal be snooping around a school on the weekend?"

"I don't know what Thurdy is up to, but you can bet we're going to find out." Jenn blew a big bubble and let it pop dramatically.

"It looks like you are going to need another writer on the newspaper to help with all of this investigating," Alex spoke up. "If you would not mind, Benji, I would be honored to be on your staff."

I didn't know what to say. Alex still seemed awfully arrogant sometimes. But he had just stood up to Thurdy for us and might have solved the whole case. He'd probably make a great reporter.

Maybe I had just been a bit intimidated by him when he showed up and seemed so worldly and knowledgeable. I smiled and stuck out my hand. "Welcome to the team, Alex. We're happy to have you on board."

With a big grin on his face, he shook my hand. "Thank you very much. I am happy to join you."

I felt a rustling on my back, then A.T. slid out of the bag and onto my shoulder. "Hey, what about me?"

"What about you, A.T.?" I asked.

"Well if all you guys are working on the paper, is there something I can do, too?" the dragon asked.

"I know!" Bonnie jumped up excitedly. "You can write an information column for the paper."

The rest of us looked at her in disbelief. "He can what?" Fred asked.

"We can call it 'Ask A.T.,'" she said, still jumping. "You know, like, 'Ask Anthony T. Dragon' himself. A.T. knows all this stuff because he's been around for so long and he's read so many books. He can answer questions about history or science or just about anything."

That actually sounded like a great idea. "What do you think, A.T.?" I asked over my shoulder.

"I think it's wonderful," he said brightly, then turned to look me in the eye. "Hey, Benji? Do you think I could get paid in granola bars?"